"Get up," Quade said in disgust.

"You were tough enough when you were manhandling the girl."

The man made no effort to move and Quade's disgust increased.

"Damn you!" a voice yelled behind him. "That's my brother."

Quade whirled around. "Your brother got the beating he deserved. You can leave it at that or we'll go on from here."

His words only infuriated the other, and Quade watched his eyes narrowly.

Then another voice shouted from across the street, "My God, no! That's Jim Quade. He'd kill you before you could get near your gun. He's the fastest draw in the West!"

Fawcett Gold Medal Books
by Giles A. Lutz:

BLOOD FEUD

RELENTLESS GUN

OUTCAST GUN

BY GILES A. LUTZ

FAWCETT GOLD MEDAL • NEW YORK

A Fawcett Gold Medal Book

Published by Ballantine Books

ISBN 0-449-12718-4

Manufactured in the United States of America

First Fawcett Crest Edition: March 1958
First Ballantine Books Edition: July 1984

ONE

JIM QUADE stopped his horse at the head of the street and looked at the town. In another hour it would be dark. Darkness would be kind to this town, hiding the paint-stripped, warped boards, the crude and hasty building. How many times had he seen this town before? Not actually this one, for the name of it was different. Except for the name it was like the countless dozens of others he had passed through—the same dusty streets, the same tired buildings lining it. The bank would be the most substantial building in town, and, he thought with a wry humor, that should teach a man something. His face hardened as he looked at the town. He wanted nothing from it except a meal or two and a night's lodging. He was a poor liar even to himself. For with each new town, a hope was stirred—a persistent hope that this town might become his own. It had been disappointed often enough to be long since dead, still it always managed to revive. How long would he stay here? An hour, a day, a week? He did not know, for it was beyond his control.

He lifted the reins and said, "Let's get you a meal, Wrangle."

The horse's weariness showed in its heavy, deliberate movements. It had hard miles behind it, not hurried, but many, and the number more than made up for speed. The man's shoulders and back were straight, though there was an aura of fatigue about him, too. It was a long time since he'd known anything but weariness, deep-down bone weariness. He rode down the street, his face straight ahead, though he caught every little movement on both sides of the street. Continuous alertness was the price of his existence, and through the years its drain bit deep. People stared at him, but he thought they showed only normal curiosity. He did not expect to find hospitality. Hospitality was a word that people knew but few really used. A stranger was always someone to be wary of.

His face looked rockhewn—harsh and bitter. He was twenty-six and looked ten years older. He seemed easy and relaxed, but the steel-spring tightness was shallow. Sweat stains showed at the armpits of his blue shirt, and a dried white band of it dipped under his belt. His jeans were covered with trail dust, and the well-worn boots were many days past a polish. The black hat was pushed to the back of his head, showing brown hair. The dust impartially filmed both hair and hat with a faint gray. His eyes were gray, shaded with blue. They were cold, unapproachable eyes, locked doors on the thoughts behind them. He wore a single gun, the black grip of it well used. His trappings were good but not flashy, and all of them showed the signs of wear. They looked like the man—worn, but still competent to do a job.

He moved down the street until he came to a livery stable. He halted the horse at its entrance, and a dirty old man pushed out of his chair and came toward him, his eyes picking up interest. Not much happened to disrupt the dull, routine hours in a small town.

Quade asked, "You got room for him?"

"Depends upon how long you're staying."

Quade swung to the ground and said shortly, "I don't know."

The old eyes were going over him, inventorying him item by item. In a younger man it would have been an affront, but the old had privileges.

The man took Wrangle's reins. "You're a stranger here, ain't you?"

"Did you ever see me before?"

The old man shook his head.

"Then you might call me a stranger."

Quade heard the man sputtering behind him as he moved away, and he allowed himself a bleak grin. That was repayment for the boldness of the old man's eyes.

He angled across the street toward the saloon sign hanging above the walk. It swung on a pipe, creaking dismally each time a breeze pushed against it. The sign and fly-specked window were labeled *The Orient Saloon*. Quade thought there must be a thousand Orient Saloons in the West. And this one would be no different in appearance from the rest of them. He hoped the liquor would be a little better than the others served.

He stepped inside, and his surmise was correct. The sawdust on the floor needed changing. It was lumpy with old dirt and dried tobacco juice, and it added its smell to the stale, liquor-laden air. The half-dozen table tops were scarred, and the chairs around them were sagging with age and use. Most of them were wired for additional support of the weary legs. The bar was battered and dull, and a man got a wavy, distorted impression of himself in the back mirror.

Four men were in the room besides the barkeep, and Quade took them in with a single quick glance which dismissed them quickly. Townsmen, he thought, stopping for a drink and a few male words before they went home for supper.

He walked to the bar, and the short, bald-headed man behind it moved to him and asked, "What'll it be, mister?"

"Whisky," Quade said. There was nothing in the room to disturb him, nothing to stir an ever-alert instinct.

The bartender poured the drink and set the bottle down. His eyes were fixed on Quade, and his lips moved, though no sound came from them.

Quade's hand stopped halfway to his lips. The instinct was alive and pulsating. "Anything wrong?" he drawled.

The bartender wet his lips and stammered, "You're— you're Jim Quade."

Quade set the glass on the bar without tasting it, sighing inwardly. He would not stay long in this town; the bartender's words were evidence of that. To the best of his knowledge he had never seen this man before, yet he had called him by name.

He said, "Maybe you're mistaken."

Excitement made the little man's eyes bug. "No, no," he said, waving his hands. "I know you. You're Jim Quade!"

Quade heard the scrape of a chair's legs and turned his head. One man was standing. All four of them stared at him with fixed fascination. He silently cursed the bartender for his memory, for blurting out his name.

"Sure you are," bartender insisted. "I saw you in El Paso. Do you think I could forget the night you killed Milo Thompson? It was right in front of my section of the bar. Milo kept prodding and prodding at you, and—"

"Shut up," Quade said.

Denial was useless. There was nothing like blood to stick an incident in a man's mind. This was only a repeat of a dozen other occasions—a faceless man remembering merely because the incident had been spectacular enough to make him remember. The past never entirely let go of a man.

Quade heard the sound of hurried footsteps and looked around again. One of the four men was just going through the swinging doors, bursting with the information that Jim Quade was in town. This was an old, monotonous pattern, and the coming events would be cut from it.

A crowd would gather outside the saloon and peer through the dirty windows, then the law would come in, sometimes nervous and blustering, sometimes calmly serious, but always demanding with the authority of the law.

He lifted his drink and tasted it. "Damn you," he said. His tone sounded almost pleasant.

The bartender backed away, his eyes wide and terrified. "I didn't mean any harm, Mr. Quade. I just recognized you, and—" His voice faded, and he kept backing away until he reached the end of the bar. His hands twisted nervously in his apron, and his eyes kept the wide fear.

Quade grunted irritably. Anyone watching this would swear the little fool expected to be shot. He finished his drink and placed the glass on the bar. The room was still—still enough for him to hear one of the men's breathing. The sound was labored and heavy. He turned around, placed his elbows on the bar, and waited. That was all that was left for him.

Two men came to the windows and peered through the dusty panes. They ducked back as they caught Quade's eyes upon them. But new arrivals emboldened them, and it was only seconds before a crowd was pressed against the windows outside. Quade's face remained wooden, but the anger was starting within him. As familiar as this was, it always angered him.

He heard the swelling of voices, coming from down the street, at first, too faint for him to distinguish words. Then as the sound came closer, he heard his name mentioned several times. The waiting was almost over.

The crowd on the walk parted to let two men through, and the doors swung open. The man in the lead was big-boned but turning to softness. His face was flushed, and his eyes were worried. Quade's eyes briefly touched the badge on the man's vest. The law was here. He put his attention on the second man. This one, too, wore a badge, and trouble could come from him. The first man had gone soft under trouble-free days, but the second one was a different caliber. He was much younger, and his lean face was stamped with a hard assurance. Quade evaluated him, and the tension began creeping along his muscles. He knew this type, those bold, hungry eyes weighing and judging him, asking, How good are you? Are you as good as they say you are?

The older man stopped three feet from Quade. He wanted to hold his eyes on Quade's face, but he could not keep them from shifting. He ran his tongue over his lower lip and said, "I'm Burt Osley. Sheriff of this country. Are you Jim Quade?"

Quade watched him with expressionless eyes. This man did not like the smell of trouble; he wanted things to stay easy and soft.

Quade did not answer, and Osley wet his lips again. His thumb and forefinger pulled at the loose flesh along his jawline, and he looked at the floor as he muttered, "This is my deputy, Stobie Hobart." He did not put the warning into exact words, but it was there. What he really meant to say and could not quite get out was, there are two of us. Don't try anything.

Hobart stood to one side of Osley, his face faintly

mocking. He, too, knew what Osley was trying to say, and he felt contempt that Osley could not put it into plainer talk. The hard, bright challenge glowed in his eyes. There was no worry in him, only an animal stalking. His arms hung at his sides, and he looked easy and relaxed, but there was tension in the fingers of his right hand.

He's probably fast, Quade thought; they usually are, when the challenge is that naked in their eyes. Hobart wanted a question answered, and there was only one way to answer it.

He put his eyes on Osley's face and said slowly, "I'm Jim Quade."

Osley sighed, the sound of a man whose fears have been realized. Men had pushed into the saloon in his wake, and he turned his head and shouted at them. "Clear out, now. All of you. Clear out." He waved his arms, and the vehemence of his words and actions were a cover for the worry Quade's admission put into him.

He looked back at Quade and asked, "Could we go to my office and talk?" An unconscious pleading was in his tone. He did not want the curious eyes of the town watching how he handled this.

Quade said, "Lead the way." Hobart remained planted, and Quade snapped, "I'll follow you."

Hobart's eyes narrowed, and a faint tinge of color touched his face. His pride had a thin and fragile crust. A word, a look, or a touch could crumble it, exposing the raw and sensitive pride.

Osley must have known about it, for he hastily placed his hand on Hobart's arm. "Come on, Stobie." The pleading was still in his voice, and Quade's evaluation was a little stronger. A sheriff did not have to beg his deputy to do anything.

Rebellion flared in Hobart's eyes, wavered, and was gone. But it was there in the man, near the surface, alive and touchy. He turned and moved out ahead of Osley.

Quade followed them out of the saloon and down the walk. Hobart's neck looked stiff and red. Quade's tone and attitude were an affront to him. But those kind could never be handled gently. They always took it as a sign of weakness.

Osley and Hobart entered a small building, at the end of the block. The letters on the window said *Sheriff's Office*. Quade knew what the interior looked liked before he stepped inside. A minimum of furniture, most of the use worn from it. The floor dirty, and the walls needing paint and partially covered with yellowing wanted posters. He was right on every detail.

Osley said, "Sit down," and his voice was too jovial.

He took the chair before the roll-top desk, and Quade sat in the remaining one. Hobart stood near the door, his eyes never leaving Quade's face.

Osley rolled a cigarette and handed the makings to Quade. Quade shook his head, and Osley tucked them back into a vest pocket. He had a smile on his face, but there was no depth to it. He asked, "You planning on staying in town long?" There was hope in the question, hope that the answer would be negative.

"That depends on a lot of things, doesn't it, Quade?" Hobart drawled.

"Can you name any of them?" Quade asked, making no attempt to disguise the insult of his tone.

Hobart flushed, and his face turned dangerous. "I might," he snapped. "Nobody here's afraid of your reputation. Maybe you ain't as good as you think you are. Eight men, isn't it? How many of them were real, and how many of them stories? Maybe stories you spread yourself."

Osley said hastily, "That damned crowd's followed us down here, Stobie. Go out and break it up."

The rebellion showed again in Hobart's eyes, but as yet it had no real strength. As he turned toward the door he cut his eyes at Quade and said, "I might be seeing you again—if you stay around."

"You might," Quade said evenly.

He watched Hobart go through the door. A big, easy-moving man with an open confidence that amounted to a swagger. You're wrong, Hobart, Quade thought. It's ten men. Two you haven't heard about. And they're all real. How very real they were. He could not put names nor places nor dates to any of them, but the faces did not fade.

Osley said, "Stobie's young and kind of hotheaded. He doesn't mean anything by it."

And he wants a reputation, Quade thought. The hunger for it was naked in Hobart's eyes. He would not get too many opportunities in a small, out-of-the-way town. Hobart would hate to see a reputation pass him by. Quade thought morosely, I wish I could give him mine.

"You figuring on staying long?" Again Osley's question, too casually put and failing to disguise his fear of a negative answer.

Quade considered the words. Sometimes they were put differently, but the meaning was always the same. Some of them asked him to go, and some demanded it, but in any case, they did not want him around. He kept silent, wanting Osley to work harder for this.

Osley turned an earnest face toward him. "We've got a peaceful town here. I want to keep it that way. But when things happen that I can't control—" He stopped and blew a lugubrious sigh.

Osley had put it into words. Something always happened if Jim Quade stayed in town. A Hobart came along, and a wrong word or a wrong movement was followed by violent action. He could understand Osley's position. Those violent actions made a sheriff's job hard.

"I'll leave when I'm ready," Quade said in a flat voice. He let the worry take Osley's features, then said with a bleak smile, "It won't be long. I want a meal, a few supplies, and a night's sleep."

"Sure, sure," Osley said with an outburst of relief. "If there's anything I can do to help, you call on me."

The relief in Osley's face told Quade the story. Here was a man growing old and needing desperately to hold his job. He wanted that job peaceful, and one of these days, that want would gobble him up. For he was not in a peaceful line of work.

Quade asked, "Hobart been working for you long?"

Osley's face looked uncertain. "Six months." He stared at Quade with puzzled eyes. "He's a good deputy," he said weakly.

"You hired him because he's young and tough," Quade said. "You hired him to keep things off you. Right now, he's satisfied with a deputy's badge. It won't last. One of these days, he'll take you over."

"Here now," Osley said in a blustering voice. He locked eyes with Quade, then stared at the wall.

"Remember it," Quade said. He swore at himself as he left the office. Why had he bothered? Deep down, Osley probably knew it as well as he did.

He paused outside and rolled a cigarette. A nameless longing was in him as he glanced up and down the street. A man needed roots, a sense of belonging. He had picked a lonesome trail, and it took the years and the experience of them to tell him just how lonesome it was.

He looked across the street and saw a restaurant. His belly rumbled. He looked back after he crossed the street. Osley stood in the doorway, watching him. Osley would not draw an easy breath until Quade left town.

"I won't keep you worrying too long," Quade called with bleak humor.

TWO

PRIAM CHESBROUGH stopped at the beam of light coming through the saloon doors. He would have to cross it, just as he crossed other beams of light—and each one was a new dread, for someone might recognize him. His heart beat painfully faster at the memory of results of past recognitions. That was why he picked this time of day to come into town—just before the stores closed. He made the trip as rarely as possible, hanging outside a store until he was sure it was empty, then hurriedly slipping in and making his meager purchases. He never visited a saloon, or any other place where men might gather, and he always tied his horse and wagon beyond the outskirts of town, hoping no one would find it before he returned. Twice they had, and his harness had been cut and the wagon damaged. He looked up at the sky and thought with a desperate urgency, Oh, God, all I ask is to be left alone.

He took a deep breath and scurried across the beam of light like a frightened animal. Even after he was across it and his pace slowed, his breathing was raspy for the remainder of the block. He did not see the man come out of the saloon and stare after him. He did not see the man's eyes shine with a cruel brightness. The man stepped back into the saloon, a hard smile on his lips.

Two women customers were in Hamilton's store, and Priam waited outside in the shadows until they made their purchases and left. He remained where he was until the echoes of their chatter faded, and the waiting had its fearful effect, for his heart was pounding and a film of sweat dampened his face. Once, he had been proud of the name Priam Chesbrough; now he cursed it. Changing it would do no good. He was too well known around here. He had one other course. He could leave.

He looked all about him, and the street was empty. He tried to straighten his shoulders as he went up the three wooden steps. He still looked bent and furtive.

He caught a reflection of himself as he passed a mirror, just inside the door. His hair was raggedy, showing the efforts of a man trying to do his own trimming. The crown of his hat was broken in front, and gray-streaked brown hair showed through the break. He needed a shave, and even the heavy beard could not disguise the fear on his face. He was forty-five, but looked older. Worry and fear aged a man beyond all natural processes. His clothes were worn and mended many times, but clean. Cleanliness was the last straw of his pride, and he fiercely clung to it. His right arm hung stiffly at his side, and the hand seemed frozen in a clawlike posture. The hand was all right for slow, routine work, but useless when speed and deftness were required.

Hamilton looked up from behind the counter and scowled. "You again," he said. His face and tone held no welcome. He was a thin, angular man with a pinched face. His lips were always pursed as though he nursed a permanent disapproval of everything he saw.

The beginning of a smile froze on Priam's face. Why did he insist upon trying to be friendly? None of these people would ever change. Hamilton only mirrored what they all felt. Priam used to rage at this attitude, but weariness and futility had burned away most of the rage, leaving only the ashes of dull acceptance. A man made a mistake, and society never forgot or forgave it.

He pulled a pencil-written list from his pocket, a list made over the passing of several weeks. An item too easily slipped away unless he wrote it down; a forgotten item could mean another trip to town, a going through the fear and worry all over again.

He looked at the list and said, "A sack of beans, flour, sugar, two pounds of coffee—" Hamilton's lack of response stopped him, and he raised his eyes. Hamilton had not moved. He stared at Priam with blank eyes.

A flash of anger appeared in Priam's eyes. "I've got the money," he growled. He pulled a soiled wad of bills from his pocket. He went through this every time. Hamilton disliked him, but the dislike didn't extend to Priam's money. He would take that readily enough.

Hamilton nodded at the sight of the money and began filling the order. The pile of items on the counter grew. It was going to be a brutally heavy load, and Priam wished he dared bring his wagon into town. He ordered few perishables, and a man grew tired of the foods that kept well. But it was either order this way or make more trips into town.

He read off the last item and said, "I guess that's it."

Hamilton added up the total and took the soiled bills. He opened a drawer, picked up a few coins, and threw them out upon the counter.

Priam picked up the coins and asked, "You got a gunny bag?" At the narrowing of Hamilton's eyes he snapped, "I'll pay for it." He dumped the coins back on the counter.

Some brief expression showed in Hamilton's eyes. If it were shame, it did not last very long, for he took the quarter, leaving a dime and four pennies. Priam's lips thinned at the outrageous overcharge, but he said nothing.

He packed the items into the gunny bag and grunted as he swung it to his shoulder. He bent under his burden as he turned toward the door. He would never be able to carry it to the wagon without several stops to rest.

He looked back from the door. He hated to leave the lights of the store, and he would have given anything for a moment of friendly conversation. He faced another lonely night in his shack. He should be getting used to them, but a man never quite seemed to arrive at that point.

He sighed and stepped through the doorway. A hard boot toe kicked into his right leg, knocking it from under him. A startled yell grabbed in his throat. He dropped the bag in an effort to save his balance, but it was too late for that. He plunged forward, getting his hands under him before he hit the porch. A jolting pain ran through the crippled arm. The knees of his trousers tore against the rough wood, and he felt sharp stabs as splinters dug into his flesh. He stopped his roll before he reached the steps, and lay there momentarily stunned. His arm and his knees hurt, and a great watery hollow was filling his stomach. He knew without looking around that the tripping was no accident.

He pushed himself up to hands and knees and slowly looked over his shoulder. He looked like a trapped animal, but there was no fight in him. A man could only take so many blows until the will to resist was beaten away.

He knew the three men well. They stood in the light from the doorway, two of them grinning at him, the older man's eyes filled with cold hatred. They were Colonel Darcy MacLendon and his two sons, Jonse and Wilkie.

Jonse was the younger, a short man barely out of his teens. He had a round, chubby face and black curly hair. He wore expensive, showy clothing and high-priced boots. His affected swagger, both in word and manner, was the result of his immaturity and of being a Mac-Lendon. He chuckled with wicked satisfaction and said, "You didn't think I saw you sneaking past the saloon, did you, Chesbrough?" He had an odd, high voice, adolescent in pitch. "Were you going to sneak out of town without saying hello to us? That ain't neighborly, Chesbrough."

He advanced a step, and Priam cowered.

"Hell," Wilkie said disgustedly. "How you going to fight something that crawls on the ground? Damn you," he said in sudden fury. "Get up. Act like a man." He took a quick step and kicked Priam in the ribs.

Priam clamped his lips against the groan that threatened to tear them open. The kick put a sickness in his stomach that rose in sour waves, gagging in his throat. He shut his eyes against the pain and did not get up. He knew what would happen, if he did—he would be knocked down again. It had happened too many times before.

Wilkie stood over him, and Priam thought he was going to kick him again. Wilkie was five years older than his brother. There was no resemblance between them. Wilkie was a good six inches taller, and his face was lean and hard. Lines of cruelty etched deep paths from his mouth corners, and his forehead always looked furrowed and mean. He was careless of appearance and dress and looked like a tramp beside his brother. Jonse was cruel much of the time because of boredom. Wilkie was cruel by nature, a deep, ingrained cruelty that struck out against man and animal.

Priam muttered, "All I'm asking is that you leave me alone."

His words only infuriated Wilkie, for he drew back his foot.

"Stop it, Wilkie," Colonel MacLendon commanded. He was almost as tall as Wilkie. His face was angular and cold. The gray goatee and mustache did not hide the thinness of mouth nor the sharpness of chin. He was rarely known to raise his voice in anger, nor show it on his face. While a man did not see anger, he always felt it was there behind the cold fastness of his eyes, and the town both feared and respected him. He was supposed to have been a Confederate officer, and people said the war had molded him out of steel.

His words might not have stopped Wilkie, but what Jonse said did. Jonse took a quick side step from his brother and said, "Whew. I just got a whiff of you. Don't you ever take a bath?" He had a child's mind, unable to hold a focal point of interest very long. Meeting no resistance in Priam, he turned his interest to bedeviling his brother.

Wilkie's face went wild with rage. Like most cruel men, he was thin-skinned to barbs directed at him. "God damn you," he roared, lunging toward Jonse. "I told you before. You keep your tongue off me."

Priam knew fresh hope. If the two fought, he might be able to pick up his bag and escape further attention from them.

The hope was instantly dashed. Colonel MacLendon stepped between his two sons. He lifted the quirt he carried and brought it down in a slashing blow across Wilkie's shoulder.

Wilkie yelped and fell back. He raised a hand to his stinging flesh, his eyes insane with fury. But he made no move toward his father. "You're always taking his side," he said sullenly. "Why don't you hit him?"

Jonse chortled and slapped his thigh. Wilkie turned those burning eyes upon him, which only made Jonse laugh harder.

"I'm taking no side," MacLendon said coldly. "You

started it. I'll stand for no fighting among ourselves." He looked at Priam and his voice was emotionless. "Get out of the country, Chesbrough. My patience is wearing thin."

Priam's eyes were filled with entreaty. "Let me alone," he begged. "I'm causing you no harm."

"You killed my brother," MacLendon said. His voice was as dispassionate as though he were announcing that tomorrow would be bright.

"I paid for it." The memory of the cost made Priam's voice tremble. He had paid for it with ten years of his life—ten of the most torturous years a man would ever know.

"You paid the court," MacLendon said. "Not me." He put a boot upon Priam's sack and ground his heel against it.

Priam heard packages split and rip, and he shouted, "Please. Don't do that."

Wilkie leaned forward and said softly, "Get up and stop him, you bastard."

Jonse's attention was refocused on Priam, and his eyes were bright with speculation. "Little, sniveling man," he said. "What happened to you? You used to try and fight us."

The sickness in Priam's eyes was comprised of many things—of shame and agony of spirit, of physical hurt and rage at himself and at them. The rage was the least of it. How could a man fight all of them? But Jonse was right. He used to try, and all it earned him was savage beating. He admitted giving up, but at least it saved him the beatings.

"Why don't you carry a gun?" Jonse asked. "Look how much quicker it would be for everybody." He slid the gun from his holster, and pointed it at Priam. He cocked an eye and said, "Boom! It'd be over just like that." His face looked hopeful, like a child's expecting a treat.

Priam tried to shrink from him, and the porch bannister stopped him. His heart pounded; no one could ever predict what either of the MacLendon boys would do.

MacLendon up-ended the gunny bag, and packages, both whole and torn, spilled onto the floor. "Put that gun away, Jonse," he snapped.

Jonse said in aggrieved tones, "Hell, Pa. I wouldn't shoot him, lessen he had a gun. You know that."

MacLendon grunted and systematically ground and stomped the packages under his boots. Flour and sugar and coffee mingled together with broken bits of beans. He raised his boot heel and brought it down upon canned goods, flattenting and bursting the cans. Tomato and peach juice ran through the pile, making it a sticky, ruined mess.

Priam closed his eyes and felt the tears, stinging hot, behind the lids. That was a month's supplies ruined, and he silently groaned at the thought of the money they cost. Maybe Jonse was right—maybe a gun would be the quickest and easiest way.

"Pa, let me kick him again," Wilkie said.

MacLendon seized their shoulders and shoved them toward the steps. He looked at Priam and said. "My God, man. You won't fight and you won't leave. What are we going to have to do?" A rare anger was visible in his jerky breathing.

He regained control and said in a flat, cold voice, "You'll be glad to leave some day, Chesbrough. You'll crawl to me and beg for a few dollars to get away on. Go on," he shouted at his watching sons. "Go on!" He followed them down the steps, his back stiff.

Priam waited until the sound of their footsteps faded. Anger filled his heart, but his face was dull. He could not meet any of them in an open gunfight. His right hand was too crippled to handle a gun, and, try as he might, he could build no speed into his left hand. The thought of bushwhacking them had entered his mind a hundred times. If he did and got all of them, he would still be hunted down like a mad dog—by the town, by the county. Sheriff Osley had promised him that, and it was no idle promise.

H E GOT to his feet slowly and looked at the door of the store. Hamilton was peering out at him. He ducked out of sight as Priam's eyes touched him.

He heard footsteps on the boardwalk and hastily jerked his head around, fearful that they were coming back. Osley came into the light and stopped with one foot on the lower step.

"What happened here?" he asked, his voice brusque. His iron-gray hair framed a hard, challenging face. He wore a vest over a collarless shirt, and the light gleamed dully from the badge pinned onto the vest. He tried to be a fair man, but circumstances and people prejudiced him.

Priam looked at the badge. It meant protection for most people, but nothing for him. "They did this," he said, and his voice was dead. He did not have to put a name to the *they*. Osley knew whom he meant.

Osley frowned at him. He wished Chesbrough would leave the county. Chesbrough was an irritant, and irritants attracted trouble. He said, "I passed the MacLendons down the street. They claimed you bumped into them and dropped your supplies."

"They lied," Priam cried. "Would just dropping them do this much damage to them?" He jerked his thumb at the mess on the porch.

Osley gave it only the briefest glance. He knew they lied, but there was no acknowledgement of it in his face.

"You want to go into court against them?" Osley asked. "Do you think a judge or a jury will take your word against theirs?"

"Hamilton saw it," Priam flared. "Ask him."

Osley looked at the doorway of the store. It was empty. "Doesn't look as if he's rushing out to testify for you," he said dryly. His eyes grew hard. "MacLendon's got a right to hate you. And the town doesn't like an ex-convict living near it. You've caused nothing but trouble ever since you came back. Why don't you get smart and leave?"

Priam said bitterly, "That's what all of you want. Give up everything to the MacLendons and go. But I won't leave."

"Then expect some more of the same," Osley said. "And don't get the idea of laying for the MacLendons. I warned you what would happen, if you did. I've warned them, too. They won't gun you, unless they find you carrying one. That's all the protection I can promise you." His eyes were remote. "The colonel is a hard man. I think he kinda likes the idea of playing with you."

Priam's left hand was clenched. He couldn't completely close the right. He was crying inside with the helplessness of total frustration.

Quade came into the light. Neither man was aware he was there until he spoke. He looked at the mess on the porch, then at the bent-shouldered man with the crippled right arm. He saw a hurt in the man's face, not a physical hurt, but a hurt of the spirit, burned deep into the lines of his face. There had been violence here a few moments ago, and Quade's curiosity was aroused. Whatever that violence had been, there was no relief for it in the stubborn set of Osley's face.

Quade asked in a soft voice, "You in trouble, old-timer?"

Both heads jerked toward him, and Quade thought he saw a brief flare of hope in the crippled man's face. If so, it was immediately washed away by dull resignation.

"No trouble," Osley said testily. "Chesbrough had a little accident. He's leaving town right away." His eyes bored into Chesbrough, and Chesbrough said dully, "I'm leaving."

Quade studied the porch. This was no accident, for boot tracks were out-lined in flour and sugar. This had been a wanton act, a deliberate trampling of a man's supplies. What had caused it Quade did not know, but it was plain to see there was no aggression in the crippled man. Yet, Osley was against him. His expression, his every word and action attested to that.

Quade said, "It looks like you do your sheriffing on one side only."

Osley's face burned a dull red. He stared at Quade for a long moment before he looked away. He said in a surly tone, "This is no affair of yours, Quade."

If the name meant anything to the crippled man, it did not show in his face. His crushed apathy made Quade want to slap him. A man should not be beaten down to such a point.

"Is it?" Osley snapped at the crippled man.

"No," Chesbrough muttered, and turned and shuffled away.

Quade didn't speak until the sound of his footsteps faded. They sounded so tired, so terribly beaten down. He put thoughtful eyes on Osley and said, "You run a right interesting town here, Sheriff. Those must be big men you're backing against a crippled man."

Osley said, "Damn it, you don't know—"

Quade cut him short. "I've seen enough to guess. You must be right proud of yourself."

He went down the walk, Osley glaring at his back.

THREE

SUSAN CHESBROUGH stepped from the stage and looked curiously at this eastern Colorado town. It looked more drab than she had remembered it, but then, a child accepted things that were a jarring affront to an adult. The business district ran for two blocks, and the street through it was unpaved, as were the other two streets of the town. The houses huddled behind the business district on either side, and she judged the town to be three or four hundred people in size. Had it grown? She couldn't remember. The buildings and houses were in sad need of painting, and she suspected the wind here was a huge scouring brush, stripping away paint almost as fast as man could put it on. A town looked so naked without paint, she thought, for without it every crack and every defect was exposed. The wood weathered to a dull uniform gray that was anything but cheery. She looked about, missing something dreadfully. Trees! That was what she missed. What trees she saw were stunted and scrubby and few and far between. No wonder the wind was a scouring brush. With nothing to break it, it could sweep its full force against this town. She thought of St. Louis and its tree-shaded streets. She would miss that part of St. Louis, but nothing else. She shut off the thought of it before any bitterness could creep into her mind.

Her face was composed, but icy tremors ran their course inside her. Perhaps she was foolish to come back here, but her desperation had driven her. The future was filled with terrifying spectres, and she tried to think of it as little as she could.

The driver was unloading her baggage from the boot, and she moved to him and asked, "Can you tell me how to reach Priam Chesbrough's place?" She should know, but it had been so many years ago that her memory was not to be fully trusted.

The driver put the last piece of luggage on the walk and straightened. He was a florid-faced man in his late

24

fifties, and the weary hours of the trail were beginning to pull at his shoulders, making them droop.

He shook his head. "I wish I could help you, ma'am. I just drive through here. I don't know too many of the people."

Any man would regret not being able to help her. She was a small woman, barely topping five feet. The hair showing beneath her bonnet was a golden mass of curls, and he had the sudden hankering to ask her to take off her bonnet. A faint grin touched his lips at the fool thought. Her eyes were a deep blue, and they had the power to look straight through a man. He would hate to have anything to hide from her. It was as pretty a face as he ever looked at, but there were shadows behind it. She was traveling with a small boy, and he suspected she had lost her husband. That was hell on a young woman.

"I'm sorry," he said again. "You ask in any of them stores. They can tell you."

He walked to the door of the stage and lifted the boy out. He was a husky youngster, maybe around five. He had his mother's curly hair, though there was more brown in it. The man noticed the eyes were the same blue. Pure hell, when a family like this had to be broken up.

He swung the boy high and held him over his head. The youngster laughed gleefully. He sat him down on the walk and said with mock ferocity, "You look out after your mother. You hear me?"

"Yes, sir," the boy said gravely.

The man nodded with approval. The youngster had manners, too.

Susan placed a hand on the driver's arm. "You have been kind to us," she said.

His embarrassment made him scowl at her, and he said a violent, "Naw!" He climbed hastily to the box and kicked off the brake. He looked down before he yelled at the teams. She looked so damned lonely standing there with the boy. It was a rough world, and his protest against it came out in his loud "Hi-yah!" at the teams.

Susan looked at the boy and said, "Jimmy, mother has to step inside this store and ask a question. You stay right here until I come back."

He said, "I will, Mommy."

She tousled his hair, feeling the lump form in her throat. Nothing would ever happen to him. The thought cut fiercely through all the other problems in her mind.

She did not want to ask in the saloon, and she passed it. She heard an outburst of men's laughter, and her lips moved with humor. Men laughed like boys, easily and raucously. Her lips lost their curve. Men could laugh easily because they rarely carried the burden a woman carried. The thought was a statement of fact, not an indulgence in weakness. It had been several years since she allowed herself the luxury of self-pity.

A woman came out of the store ahead of her. She put disinterested eyes on Susan, then her head swiveled for a longer look. She was a woman of ample proportions, and the heat of the late afternoon sun had flushed her face, which stiffened and seemed to grow more red. She moved a couple of steps nearer, and her chin quivered with self-righteous indignation.

"I know you," she said shrilly. Her eyes were hot with accusation. "I saw you and heard about you, while I was visiting in St. Louis."

Susan's face blanched. "You're—you're mistaken," she said in a small voice.

"Oh no, I'm not," the woman said, the satisfaction in her voice reflected in her face. "Do you think I could forget your kind?" She shook a plump finger in Susan's face, and her eyes were mean. "Did you think you could come out here and hide your shame? This is a respectable town. We won't have your kind around here."

Susan flung out a hand and said, "Please!"

Neither the word nor the gesture had any effect upon the woman. She turned and waddled down the walk. Her haste indicated she couldn't wait to spread the news.

TEARS stung Susan's eyes. After all those miles, almost the first person she saw in this town knew her background. The unfairness of it welled a rebellious crying into her throat, but she wouldn't give way to weakness. She brushed the tears from her eyes and straightened her shoulders. The past was never really buried. Some thread of it always remained, ready to trip a person, when they were the most unsuspecting.

A man stood on the porch of the store, curiously

watching her. He wore an apron and sleeve protectors, and she thought he must own the store, for no clerical help would be so openly loafing between customers.

As Susan came up the steps he asked, "What was Mrs. Wilson so upset about?"

"I don't know," she said in a low voice. She was grateful he had stood too far away to hear the conversation. At least for the moment, he did not know. She thought bitterly that that would not last long. She knew Mrs. Wilson's kind.

The man naming the woman placed her for Susan. While she lived in St. Louis, Mrs. Wilson visited relations across the street. Susan never met, or even talked to her, but each time she passed down the street, she was aware of the furtive glances from the house across from her, and she was quite sure tongues wagged about her.

She looked longingly down the street. The stage was out of sight, and the dust of its passage had settled. She wished she were on it, heading any place. It would do no good, she thought miserably. The threads of the past were strewn everywhere.

The storekeeper asked, "What can I do for you?"

She turned her head and caught his eyes going furtively over her. She kept her face expressionless. Those eyes would be bolder after he learned what Mrs. Wilson knew.

She asked, "Can you tell me how to get to Priam Chesbrough's place?"

His face froze, and he stared hard at her. "Ask at the livery stable," he said curtly. "Maybe they can tell you." He turned abruptly and entered the store.

Her eyes were bewildered as she watched him leave. One moment he was almost fawning over her, and the next he treated her like an untouchable. The name Chesbrough seemed to cause the change in his attitude. She felt the weakness of tears in her eyes again. Chesbrough seemed to be an unfortunate name.

She walked half a block to the livery stable and repeated her request. The old man looked at her for a long time before he spat tobacco juice into the dust. He said, "I'll drive you out there. It'll cost you ten dollars."

It seemed an outrageous charge, but she stifled her

protest. At the moment, she would pay anything to get away from this town.

She nodded, but the old man stood made no further movement. He was a dirty old man, his shirt looking as though it had not been changed for weeks. Tobacco juice streaked his chin, turning the beard yellow.

She did not like his eyes, and she said in quick exasperation, "I want you to drive me there."

The old man growled, "I'm waiting for my pay."

She flushed and dug in her handbag. She pulled out two bills from her diminishing supply and placed them in his hands. He stuffed them into his pocket, grunted, and walked into the stable.

Susan twisted the strap of her bag. There was insult in his eyes and in the way he asked for payment in advance, but she could do nothing about it.

He came back, driving a dilapidated wagon and a sorry horse. She pointed to the boy and her baggage, down the street. He grunted and drove to the spot, letting her walk. He made no move to help her place the bagage in the wagon, and she thought of the stage driver and his kindness.

She lifted the boy into the seat and climbed up beside him, her chin stiff. Each contact with this town seemed to be worse than the last.

Sнɛ stared straight ahead, thinking of the coming meeting with Priam Chesbrough. So much depended upon his reactions.

The boy talked about everything they passed, and the old man growled, "Shut up. If there's anything I can't stand, it's a chattering kid."

Susan placed an arm about Jimmy and drew him to her. Her eyes flashed at the old man, and she murmured in Jimmy's ear, "It's all right, darling." She wanted this ride over, and she asked, "How far is it?"

The old man spat over a wagon wheel and said, "About ten miles." He cut his eyes at her and asked, "What's Chesbrough to you?"

She said stiffly, "He's my father."

"Thought there was some relation," the old man grunted. "You'll be sorry for that."

She would not allow the questions in her mind to be spoken; she would not ask anything of this man. . . .

SHE thought the trip would never end. It took the horse the better part of two hours, and she wanted to scream at its slowness. The old man finally stopped the wagon and said, "We're here. That's it."

She knew dismay as she looked at it. The tarpaper shack sat some three hundred yards from the road, looking bleak and desolate. She had lived here as a child, but surely it could not have been this awful. There was a noticeable sag in the roof, and the whole house looked too tired to stand. A piece of tarpaper was off on the west end, showing gaping cracks in the boards beneath it. The outbuildings were as bad. Everything showed neglect and a sense of futility. The ground around the buildings was parched and barren under the summer sun, and the purple mass of the mountains, rising far off in the distance, could do nothing to soften the scene. It was unfriendly and foreboding, and a shudder ran through her.

She waited for the old man to turn off toward the house, and he said, "Ain't driving onto his place."

Her lips were a thin line as she climbed out of the wagon. She lifted Jimmy to the ground, then walked to the rear of the wagon and removed her baggage.

She came back and said, "I'm so grateful to you for all your kindness."

The barb did not penetrate. "You won't be," the old man said. He slapped the ancient horse with the reins and yelled, "Giddap."

Susan's heart pounded as she looked at the house. Fear was mounting inside her. She looked at the wagon and was tempted to call it back. But she knew that even if the old man heard her, he would not return. He had been in such haste to get rid of her.

She took a deep breath and said, "Jimmy, stay here. Mommy will be right back for you." She did not know how well founded her words were. Perhaps her baggage would get no closer to the cabin than it was right now.

She trudged up the dusty lane leading to the house. A few chickens picked dispiritedly at the scant vegetation, and the yard was littered with pieces of broken machinery and boards. She stepped up onto the porch, and its cracked boards groaned under her weight. Her mouth was dry, and she could have made no sound, if she wanted to. She almost hoped he was not home.

She did not have to knock, for the front door was open. She saw a man sitting inside the room. His shoulders were bent, and he stared blankly at the floor. The side view of his face was familiar, but he looked so different, he looked so old. Eleven years changed everything with a relentless hand.

She said in a small voice, "Father?"

He turned his head and stared at her.

She stepped inside and asked, "Have you forgotten me?"

He got up as though he were sleepwalking and came toward her. His voice trembled as he said, "It's Susan, isn't it?"

He opened his arms, and she ran into them. She put her face against his chest and cried, and by the shaking in his body she thought he was crying, too.

He pushed her to arm's length, and his hands held her as though afraid she would disappear. He looked long at her, and his eyes were moist. He said in a wondering voice, "I'd know you anyplace. You look just like her." He hugged her again and said in an unsteady voice, "I never figured on seeing either of you again. You don't hate me, do you, Susan?"

She pulled away and looked into his face. It came to her with a small marveling that he needed comforting and consoling even more than she did.

She said gently, "Mother didn't hate you, Father. Before she died she talked a lot about you. I didn't know until a few months ago that you were—" her voice broke, then steadied—"freed. It was bad, wasn't it?"

He looked at the far wall with blank eyes, and she knew he stared into the past. "It was bad," he said somberly. "You were pretty young when it happened. How much of it do you know?"

She started to say "Enough," then saw he needed to talk. She sat down and waited for him to begin.

"I was thirty-four when it happened, Susan," he said in a faraway voice. "Crazy in love with your mother. Too crazy, I guess." His voice faded until she could scarcely hear it. "My jealousy made both of us miserable. I couldn't stand to have other men even look at her. I thought one man in particular was paying her too much attention. We made a trip to Arizona, and he showed up there. She had nothing to do with it, but I accused her of it. I provoked him into a fight and killed him." His left hand was tightly clenched, the right rested upon his knee. "He was too drunk to really defend himself. Some said it was murder. Maybe I'd have been better off if the judge saw it that way. He called it manslaughter and gave me ten years in Yuma. Do you know what that means?"

She could not trust herself to speak. She mutely nodded.

He looked at her with unseeing eyes. No one who had never been in Yuma could know what it was like. Pitiless heat in summer and cold in winter so severe that a man's bones felt as though they were cracking. Cells carved out of solid rock, with roofs ten feet or more thick. Each cell was secured with double-grilled iron doors set four feet apart. No desperate or crazed inmate could reach out and grab a passing guard. The place was staffed with inhuman guards, who forced men to work bareheaded in the summer Arizona sun, when they longed for the coolness of those rocky cells. The food was not fit for hogs, and beatings were liberally applied. It was little wonder that many men went crazy after a few months of such treatment.

He said dully, "No one could know. Men wanted to die there. You'd sit and think about the cemetery on the rocky hill overlooking the river, and it seemed a good place to be. I saw men go screaming crazy. Crazy enough to rush the main gate trying to use their bare hands against armed guards." He lifted his right hand. "I was one of them. A bullet smashed the bones. They didn't care how it healed."

"Don't," she said in a choking voice. "It's all behind you now."

"Is it?" he asked roughly. He shook his head, a slow, despairing gesture. "Nothing's ever really over. The man I killed was Carter MacLendon. Do you remember the MacLendons? Wilkie used to make you cry, when you were little."

She vaguely remembered him. Wilkie was a dirty boy with a dirty mind. She had always been afraid of Wilkie's cruelty. There was another one, but she could not recall his name. He had been much younger than Wilkie, barely able to toddle after him.

She said in a whisper, "I remember them."

Priam's face twisted with a spasm of emotion. "The MacLendons were always big people around here. They could do anything, and everyone excused them. Carter MacLendon was Colonel Darcy MacLendon's brother. People around here think it's because of his brother that Darcy MacLendon hounds me. It isn't. Don't you remember how he was grabbing everything before we went to Arizona?"

He shook his head. "No, you wouldn't remember. You were too little. He's always been a land-hungry man. He used this land while I was gone, and he doesn't want to give it up. He's using the past to drive me away. Just two sections of land and a spring, but he wants it. People think he hates me because of his brother, and that justifies everything he does to me." In a brittle voice he told her what had happened the night before. "I can't stand up against the three of them without a gun. If I carry one, they'll kill me. I've thought of bushwhacking them. How many times I've thought of it! But I went to prison once for killing a man." His voice was almost inaudible. "I'd never go back, Susan, for any reason. I'd die first. This land is the last thing in the world I have. I swore I'd hang onto it. But I'm ready to run now. Nothing's worth being alone and hated."

She said quietly, "You're not alone. You have me."

His face was incredulous as he stared at her. "You'd stay, Susan? You'd stay with me after everything that's happened, knowing that everybody around here hates you because your name is Chesbrough?"

She said, "If you'll let me." Now was her time to talk, and she dreaded it. Her voice faltered as she said, "I brought my son with me."

His face brightened. "A son. Well, I'll be dog-goned. And I never knew anything about it. Did your husband come with you? How old is the boy?" He grinned with delight. "What do you know about that? I'm a grand-pappy."

She stared at her clasped hands in her lap. "I never had a husband."

For a moment, she thought her voice had been too low for him to hear, then he said, "Ah." The word told her nothing. The silence grew heavy in the room. Then he said, "Maybe you'd better tell me about it."

She lifted her head, and her face looked as though it were carved from marble. "I fell in love with a sick man. How sick, neither of us knew." That was not quite true. Deep down, she thought she had known—or at least suspected. "It seemed little enough to give him." She could look back without the stabbing hurt. Even now, she could not say how much of it had been love and how much the maternal instinct to shelter and comfort someone. The idyllic four-month period seemed unreal now. Would she go through it again? She could not say. It was a different time, and each time formed its own decisions.

"I left St. Louis," she said, "because other children were beginning to be cruel to Jimmy. It may follow us here." She could not tell him about Mrs. Wilson; she could not tell him that it already had.

He reached out and took her hand, and there were tears in his eyes. "How old is the boy?"

"Four," she said.

The crippled fingers held her hand, and there was strength in them. She kept her face impassive. The strength could mean several things—anger and humiliation or pity and love. She was afraid to choose, and she waited.

"You were seventeen," he said fiercely. "And alone. You were nothing but a baby yourself. It's all part of the mistake I made. If I'd been around, none of it would have happened."

She knew she was going to cry. He knew it, too, for he said, "I want to see my grandson."

He strode to the door, and she used the interval to wipe her eyes. The two of them needed each other equally. She heard him yell, "Jimmy! Get up here and see your grandpappy."

She thought of Mrs. Wilson. There would be difficulties ahead, but it was not going to be as hard as it once was. It was never as hard as when one stood alone.

Priam looked around and said, "Were you afraid I'd blame you, after the mistake I made?" He shook his head and his voice roughened. "I've got a lot to make up to you. And after last night, I can't even give you and Jimmy a decent meal."

"Have you a way to get to town?" she asked.

"I've got a horse and wagon."

Her chin was high and determined. "I'll go after supplies. They won't bother me."

She saw something in his face and thought he was going to refuse to let her make the trip.

"I spent all the money I had last night," he said.

That was shame she saw in his face, and she laughed at it. "Money," she scoffed. "I have a little. That's going to be the least of our worries."

He hugged her tight, and she knew he did not want her to see his face. A man never liked a woman to see him weep. Her arms tightened about him. She prayed money would be the least of their worries.

FOUR

THE TOWN looked no more attractive to Quade the next morning. The day was already hot, and by noon the sun would be a brutal club, hitting man and animal alike until movement under it would be held to the least possible effort. He should have been gone several hours ago, and he absently swore at his late awakening. It had been a long time since he permitted himself that luxury. But the old thoughts had kept him awake last night, building a weariness that reached deeper than he realized. Even his mind was tired, and when a man reached that stage, it took him a long time to come back.

He rolled a cigarette, noting that there was only enough left in the sack for one more. He needed tobacco, and he should be thinking about what other supplies he would take with him. He would leave this town after dark, when it was relatively cool after the heat of the day. Osley would be miserable, he thought with sardonic amusement, for he would have the rest of this day to sweat through. He had watched Quade enter his room last night, and he had been waiting in front of the hotel, when Quade came out this morning. He had sat across the restaurant as Quade ate breakfast, only picking at his own food. There was nothing subtle about him—he was openly riding herd on potential trouble, trying to keep it in bounds, hoping to keep away any irritating factors that might cause an explosion.

Quade wondered where Osley had sent Hobart, for he had not seen the man around. He guessed Osley had gotten Hobart out of town on some pretext, and that was smart on Osley's part and a relief to Quade. Hobart would have pried and poked and prodded, and under this heat it would not have taken much to rasp any man's temper. Quade learned long ago that a man's good nature was tied to a thermometer. The higher the temperature went, the more it sucked a man's tolerance from him.

35

He threw away the half-smoked cigarette and rolled another, twisting the ends of the brown paper deep, for the tobacco was scanty. He threw away the empty sack and cut across the street toward the general store.

The stain of last night's mess was still visible on the porch, and Quade glanced at it as he stepped through the door. He remembered the beaten attitude of the crippled man and frowned. A man should be able to hold up his head. When pride was taken from him, he had nothing left.

He ordered three sacks of tobacco and stuffed them into his pocket. "You have some trouble last night?" he asked the storekeeper.

"We had some trouble here, but I wasn't in on it," the man answered. "It was that damned Chesbrough's fault. He caused it, and I had to clean up the mess he left."

Chesbrough! That was the name Osley called the man with the crippled arm. From the storekeeper's vehemence Quade could be wrong about who was the aggressor in the affair.

He asked with mild interest, "What happened?"

"He got in an argument with Colonel MacLendon and his two sons. He's always at it."

"Ah," Quade said softly. Perhaps he was not so far wrong in his first judgment. It would be hard to make a case of aggression in a crippled man against three.

"The MacLendons stomp his supplies?"

"They did," the storekeeper said with malicious satisfaction. He saw a subtle hardening in Quade's face and said, "Chesbrough had it coming. The Colonel owes him a lot more than just tromping his supplies. If Chesbrough was smart, he would leave now, while he's able to leave. No, sir," he said vigorously. "I don't blame the colonel for anything he does to Chesbrough."

Osley had shone this same atttiude toward the crippled man last night, and Quade suspected that if he sampled the town, the attitude would be general. Quade had seen this before. For some real or fancied reason, a group of people became set against one, and they were as savage as a flock of chickens pecking away at another that had been injured. Usually, the pecking kept up until the injured one was dead. He felt anger stir within him.

He knew what it was to be alone and bucking the high, hard wall of public disapproval.

He said, "The MacLendons must be big people here."

"The biggest," the storekeeper said, an unconscious tinge of pride in his voice, as though he were proud to be a part of a community that held the MacLendons.

Quade had never seen the MacLendons, but an opinion of them was already formed. Three men did not maliciously abuse a lone, crippled man. A quarrel was one thing, with its results hot and conclusive, but from what he gathered, this abuse had been going on for some time.

He snapped, "How often do they make you shine their boots?"

The storekeeper's jaw went slack as he digested Quade's words, then his face turned crimson. "You be careful how you talk about the MacLendons," he said indignantly. "Let me tell you—"

"Save it," Quade said brusquely. He threw some coins down upon the counter. The temperature must be higher than he suspected, for his temper seemed awfully thin.

He turned his head at the rumble of wheels, sounding from the street. A battered wagon drew up before the store, and a woman jumped down and tied the tired, old horse to the hitch-rail. Her hasty actions amounted almost to furtiveness, and Quade's interest sharpened.

The storekeeper said, "You ought to find out a few things before you take a side. That's the Chesbrough girl. I could tell you some thing about her, too."

Quade's eyes blazed at him, stopping the morsel of local gossip the man was chewing on. Damn a small town, Quade thought. It pried and dug into an individual's life, and rarely was that interest based on kindness.

He did not get a full look at her until she came through the door. She was very young, he thought, and she had the loveliest face Quade had seen for many a month, and the appeal in it touched him. This girl was frightened and trying hard not to show it. But it was in the heightened color that touched her cheekbones, in the quick way her eyes touched first him, then the storekeeper, then moved away.

She came toward the counter, and Quade stepped aside for her. He glanced at the storekeeper, and he wanted to knock the damned judging look from his face.

The girl pulled a list of items from her handbag and said in a breathless voice, "Please. May I have these things?"

The storekeeper made no move, and her eyes lifted to his face. Color grew in her cheeks, and she placed money beside her list. No words were exchanged, but the subtle insult was there. Quade's anger grew as he speculated upon how often she was subjected to this kind of insult.

The storekeeper moved with deliberate slowness, enjoying his upper hand. His eyes kept raking her, and there was a nasty, pointed ugliness in them. Some common knowledge was shared between them, for the misery grew in her face.

"Fill that order," Quade growled. "I want some things."

Her startled eyes went to his face, then moved away. They were blue eyes, the shade of a clear mountain morning. It was a crime and a waste for a woman's eyes to carry the shadow hers did.

The storekeeper moved under Quade's hard stare. He muttered to himself in a voice too low for Quade to catch, but he filled the order.

Quade debated upon offering to carry her sack to the wagon, then decided against it. She was already hurting from some inner embarrassment, and the kindest thing was to let her slip quietly away.

He waited until the door closed behind her before he turned to the storekeeper. He said, "You need some mannering."

The storekeeper swelled with indignation, but his eyes would not meet Quade's. He muttered, "If you knew what I know about her—"

Quade said, "You miserable son of a bitch." He despised a man who set his mind or words against a woman.

He ached for the man to resent the insult, but outside of the color mounting in the man's face, there was going to be no other show of resentment.

He heard the scuffling of feet from the porch and

jerked his head around. He heard the girl say in a quick, frightened voice, "Let go of me."

He started toward the door, and the storekeeper said with malicious satisfaction, "Now, meddle in it. That's Wilkie MacLendon out there."

Quade put a burning glance on him and stepped to the screen door. The girl was trying to hold her sack of groceries in one hand, while trying to tug the other one free. The other was pinioned in a tall man's grip. Fright and anger showed on her face. "Let go of me," she panted, jerking violently on her hand.

"Now, Susan," Wilkie said in a coaxing voice. "That ain't no way to act to an old friend." His attention was absorbed in the girl; he did not see Quade step out of the door.

His strength was far superior, and he drew the girl toward him. She dropped her sack, and it split against the porch. Smaller packages and cans rolled over the wooden surface. It left a hand free, and she used it to slap him. Quade heard the sharp report as her hand landed against his cheek.

It did not make Wilkie released his grip, but the pupils of his eyes grew smaller as he swore. He had the meanest pair of eyes Quade ever saw. The iris was abnormally large, and tawny as an owl's. The pupils were small and black and bright with some wicked inner fire.

"Hell," Wilkie said in a gusty voice. "Don't try to play that on me." He drew her close and wrapped both arms about her. "I heard all about you. You been doing things since old Wilkie saw you last. You ain't so hard to get."

The beard stubble on his chin was only a few inches from her face, when Quade seized his shoulder. Wilkie uttered a startled oath as Quade's fingers bit deep. His arms fell away from the girl, and Quade spun him. He hit him flush in the mouth before the shock of the unexpected interruption was fully planted on his face.

THE force of the blow knocked Wilkie against the wall of the store. His arms flung wide, and for a moment, he was spread-eagled against the rough boards. He waved his arms to hold his balance, but his knees buckled, and he went down hard.

Quade heard the sound of the girl's running feet down

the steps, but he did not look around. Wilkie MacLendon wore a gun, and the dazed expression on his face was changing to one of murderous fury.

Quade called a "Wait," after her. The word did not stop her, for shortly after, he heard the pound of hoofs and the rumble of wheels.

He kept his eyes fixed on Wilkie. As soon as Wilkie's head fully cleared, he would claw for that gun.

"Why, God damn you," Wilkie shouted. He grabbed at the butt of the gun, and his rage and awkward position made his movement clumsy. Quade watched him with detachment. If Wilkie could do no better than that, he was a damned fool ever to reach for a gun. He waited until the gun was clear of the holster, then stepped in and swung his boot. Wilkie yelped with pain as the toe thudded into his wrist. His hand flew up, the fingers opened, and the gun arched across the porch, landing on the street side of the bannister. He held his throbbing wrist, and his early hate was mild compared to what was in his eyes now.

"Get up, Wilkie," Quade begged. He did not want to kill this man—that would have been too easy for Wilkie and over too quickly. He wanted to punish him, to cut and tear his face, so that in the slow healing of the wounds, Wilkie would have many reasons to remember this incident.

Wilkie came up off the floor, and Quade gave him no credit for that. Most men would get up once. Would Wilkie come back after the second or third flooring? Quade would judge him after that.

He heard the pound of running feet in the street, making a heavier sound than the girl's had made, and he knew other people were running to the scene. This violence was only seconds old, yet people were drawn to it. They seemed to smell it, just as flies smelled blood.

Wilkie dived at him, his arms flung wide. He was an awkward man. This was going to be no fight; this was only going to be brutal punishment.

Quade stepped inside the wide-spread arms, feeling the inside of Wilkie's forearm brush his shoulder. He slugged him in the belly, and Wilkie's breath left him in a gasping, choked grunt. He bent over double, his arms wrapped around his belly, uttering guttural animal sounds as he fought for breath. Quade lifted his knee and caught Wilkie full in the face with it. That knee-lift was a brutal thing—it could smash every bone in a man's face; it could literally tear off his head. But Quade softened it at the last second. He wanted Wilkie hurt, hurt mad enough to come back for more, not stretched unconscious on the porch.

The impact straightened Wilkie and threw him backward. He lit on his shoulder blades, and his head made a distinct thud as it struck the floor. He lay on his back, his hands making feeble, pawing motions beside him. His eyes were hazy and streaming water; his nose spurted blood and was oddly askew. Quade hoped it was broken.

"Get up, Wilkie," he said. "We've just started." He watched the other with cold, clinical detachment. Now, he would see just how much man lay on the floor. Wilkie was not hurt badly. He was bloody, and his eyes swam in water, but nothing was broken—unless it was the nose, and that would not impair his fighting ability.

Wilkie made no effort to get up. He made a little moaning sound.

Quade shook his head in disgust. Wilkie had no intention of trying to rise. He said, "Get up, you bastard. You were tough enough when you were manhandling the girl."

He kicked Wilkie in the side, not to gently, and Wilkie's moaning grew in volume.

Quade's disgust increased. Wilkie's punishment was at an end, unless Quade wanted to kick him into insensibility. He was tempted; he even drew back his boot.

"Damn you," a voice yelled from behind him. "Don't you kick my brother."

He whirled and was startled at the size of the crowd. It packed the walk before the store, and he could feel its hostility flowing toward him. He easily picked out the man who yelled at him, picked him out by the fury that twisted his face. The man was barely out of his teens, and his face was flushed with anger, his body tensed with fury. He was no gunfighter, Quade thought. He wore the holster too high and too far forward, and in that position, it would fight the metal slipping from it. Also, he had not cleared his own position. The crowd hemmed him in and would hamper his arm movements. Even as Quade analyzed him, he remembered that voice—high and oddly shrill, like an excited kid's. Rage and excitement, Quade thought, probably made the voice break like that. A tall, thin man stood beside the younger man, an older man with a goatee and a cold, haughty face. Quade caught the resemblance between the two, and he thought, they're all here—the three Mac-Lendons the storekeeper spoke of.

He said, "Your brother earned what he got. You can drop it, or pick it up."

His words further inflamed the young man's face. He was picking it up—it was in the fury of his eyes.

"Jonse," Osley yelled. "My God, no! That's Jim Quade."

Quade picked up the sheriff out of the corner of his eye. Osley stood a dozen feet from Jonse, and his face was heavy with worry.

The name meant nothing to Jonse, but it did to the older man beside him. He grabbed Jonse' gun hand and struggled with it as Jonse tried to throw him off. Osley parted the men between them and came to the older man's assistance. He jerked Jonse's gun out of its holster and threw it into the street. He panted, "Jonse, listen. He'd kill you before you could touch it. That's Jim Quade. The fastest gun in the country."

His words penetrated the raging fog in Jonse's mind. He still struggled, but the heart was gone out of it.

Osley said, "Go on down the street, Jonse. Have a drink and cool off."

Jonse let two men lead him away, and before he went a dozen feet, he turned his head and yelled, "I ain't forgetting this."

Quade let it pass. It was said in bravado for the benefit of the crowd.

The older man came up the steps, and Osley fell in behind him like a well-trained dog.

The older man put a glance on Wilkie, who still lay on the floor. There seemed to be no particular interest in it, yet when he looked at Quade, Quade saw the coldest pair of eyes he'd ever looked into.

The man said, "What's all this about?"

Quade said, "Your son was manhandling a woman."

Osley said in a blustering voice, "Quade, if you think you can go around here starting trouble wherever you want to, you got—"

The older man waved him quiet. His eyes had never left Quade's face. The closing of the door broke his attention. He turned his head and looked at the storekeeper. He said, "Hamilton, what happened?"

Hamilton said, "Colonel, the Chesbrough girl was in here. When she left, Wilkie spoke to her, and—"

Quade saw the man intended disguising Wilkie's part in this. "Tell him what happened!" he snapped.

Hamilton's eyes broke before Quade's hard gaze. He said reluctantly, "Well, Wilkie did get kinda rough."

MacLendon's eyes went back to Quade's face. His voice had the clipped edge of a man used to giving orders and receiving obedience. "You stepped into something that didn't concern you. I'll put it down to ignorance and forgive it this once. My advice to you is to leave this town as quickly as possible."

Quade drawled, "Colonel, I never found unasked-for advice worth a damn." He put deliberate affront into his tone. He saw the man's face stiffen and just a tiny tinge of color touch the cheekbones.

Nothing showed in MacLendon's voice. "Have it your way," he said.

Quade thoughtfully regarded him. Any man who could control his emotions this well was a dangerous one.

MacLendon turned his head and looked at Wilkie. "Get up," he snapped.

Wilkie got to his feet and wiped his nose. His eyes touched Quade, then slid away. He followed his father down the steps.

He'll get some kind of hell, Quade thought. Wilkie had shamed MacLendon before the watching crowd, and to a man of MacLendon's pride, that was unbearable.

Osley yelled at the crowd, "Break it up. Go on, now. Clear out." When the last of the stragglers started away, he muttered, "Quade, you shouldn't have jumped Wilkie."

Quade said in a soft voice, "Sheriff, you heard what Hamilton said. I think less of you every time I talk to you."

Osley's face went a deep red, and his voice dropped a notch. "I'm just trying to keep peace in this town."

"You're not keeping peace. You're buying it," Quade said. He shook his head. "And what it's costing you is too big a price for a man to have to pay."

He turned his head toward Hamilton and said, "Get another sack and pick up these things."

Osley's face filled with instant alarm. "What are you intending to do?"

"I'm going to deliver these things to her."

"Don't do it," Osley said earnestly. "Quade, you don't know both sides of this. Don't push Colonel MacLendon any further."

Quade looked at Hamilton, who was staring wide-eyed at them. "Move," he snapped.

Hamilton scuttled through the door. He came back with a sack and began picking up the scattered items.

Quade put a long look on Osley and said, "You're right. I don't know both side. But I like the other one a hell of a lot better than the one you're backing."

He took the sack from Hamilton and went down the steps. He would ask his directions to the Chesbrough place from someone else.

FIVE

QUADE judged Chesbrough's place to be close to a dozen miles from town. He pulled up and frowned at the litter in the yard around the shack. He was an orderly man, and he liked to see things neat. But he could understand the litter. A lone, harassed man would put little thought to neatness. Self-respect came before neatness, and somewhere along the line, Chesbrough had lost the first.

He ground-reined Wrangle and moved the twenty-five yards to the house on foot. His face was meditative. Returning the girl's groceries was some kind of a gesture—he could not put an exact explanation to it, yet. And he would not attempt to say how far he was going beyond the gesture.

He stepped up onto the porch and stepped over a gaping hole where a board had rotted away. He heard voices coming from the interior of the house, and he moved to the door and shamelessly listened. A man could learn a great deal about people when they thought they were not overheard.

"It was awful," he heard the woman say. "If this man had not stopped him, I don't know what I would have done."

"That damned Wilkie," a man said in a dull voice. "None of them will let us alone."

Quade's eyes narrowed. There was complaint in the voice and not much anger.

Her voice was bitter as she said, "Mrs. Wilson didn't waste any time, Father. Wilkie knew. Men are worse than women. Women talk, but men try to do something."

"I ought to kill him," the man muttered.

Quade shook his head. That was said as a speculation, not as a determination. What kind of a man was this Chesbrough?

"I didn't even wait to thank the man who helped me," she said in a low voice.

"Maybe you can say it now," Quade drawled, stepping into the doorway.

She uttered a startled cry, and the man jerked around in his chair to look at Quade. His face looked belligerent enough as he asked, "Who are you? What are you doing here?"

"The name's Quade." He handed the sack of groceries to her. "I'm not rightly sure what else I'm doing here." His eyes lingered on her face. A beautiful woman, but one with trouble in her life. It left a wound in her eyes, dulling the brilliance that should be there. There was fright in the intensity with which she watched him, and he knew pity for her. She was too young to have known the rough times that marked her.

"You going to ask me in?" he asked.

"Why, yes," she said uncertainly. "Won't you come in?"

The man did not rise or speak, and the momentary belligerence was gone. Quade wondered if there were any real spirit left in him. Right now, he would say his gesture was foolish, that the ride out here was wasted. A man could help someone only if he wanted to be helped.

She asked, "Won't you sit down?"

Quade shook his head. He doubted he would be here long enough to make it worth while.

Chesbrough said, "I'm grateful for what you did for Susan."

His tone did not sound grateful. It sounded as though he were really past caring what happened. Quade briefly looked at her. Susan. It was a nice name.

"You wouldn't have done it, if you'd known what you was getting into," Chesbrough said.

Quade's eyes hardened. Damn that whining note. "Go on," he said.

"You hit Wilkie MacLendon. And you helped a Chesbrough. That ruined you around here, mister."

"Go on," Quade said again. He wanted to hear all of Chesbrough's side.

Chesbrough told him about the old killing, he told him of the MacLendon abuses and his helplessness to resist them. "They're big, and everybody bows down to them," he said dispiritedly. "They used my land while

I was gone. They don't give up anything they get their hands on. MacLendon offered me about a tenth of what my place's worth. When I wouldn't sell, he set out to drive me off. But this land is the last thing I've got."

There had been spirit in this crippled man, but had it all been pounded away. Quade could understand a man's being so hard-pressed that he did not know which way to turn, but he could not forgive a man's giving up. Maybe he had ridden out here because in the back of his mind was the thought of doing something for these people. But when the fire was out, it was futile to try helping a man. It didn't look as though there was a spark left in Chesbrough. Quade thought wryly, Maybe I came out here because they're outcasts—the same as me. Maybe I hoped I'd found a place where I finally belonged. He guessed he was wrong.

He said harshly, "When a man fights for his land, that's one thing. But no land's worth crawling for."

Chesbrough gave him a hard stab of his eyes, and there was fire in them. Quade looked at the girl, and her face was angry. His interest was reviving. Maybe he was wrong about there being no fire left in them.

He stared coldly at the man. "Even a whipped dog won't hide behind its pups." He watched with mounting interest. Chesbrough's cheeks flamed scarlet. For an instant, the man looked stunned, then fury engulfed him. He shoved at the table, pushing it from him. He got to his feet and bellowed, "Damn you!" He rushed at Quade, and a corner of the table jabbed him in the thigh. He cursed it and Quade in the same breath.

Quade heard her move and turned his head. She seized a rifle from the rack of horns on the wall and pointed it at him.

Quade said gently, "You forgot to pump a shell in." He reached out and took the rifle from her. Chesbrough was moving toward him, and Quade noticed the right fist would not completely close.

He said, "Hold it," and knew a great sense of satisfaction. Chesbrough was still part man. He took abuse from the MacLendons and the town, but that was a rut into which his thinking had fallen. A man blamed himself for something, and anything that logically stemmed from that selfblame, he accepted as being his due. It was that way with Chesbrough and the MacLendons. But he reacted violently to abuse from a stranger.

Quade said, "I was just trying to find out if there was anything left in you worth helping."

He saw the bewildered expressions on their faces. He felt good inside, a feeling he had not known for a long time. He said, "The name Quade didn't mean anything to you. It did in town. It did to Osley and the colonel." Maybe the name was good for something. Maybe it could stand as a sort of bulwark for these two. He went on, "I don't like to see people like the MacLendons push other people around—if there's any gumption left in those people."

They understood nothing of what he was saying, and his tone roughened. "From what I picked up in town, you two are outcasts. I guess I'm one, too." He grinned bleakly. "An animal maverick is valuable. A human maverick ain't worth a damn to anyone—including himself." He was making a mess out of this. He was trying to explain something, and the words were all tangled. What he wanted to say was that when a human maverick wasn't accepted by anyone, he turned to other mavericks, and in the banding together gained a certain solidarity. And perhaps that was the first step back. It was in his head, but there was no path to his tongue.

He said harshly, "I killed a man when I was nineteen. A man with a reputation as a gun. It was a fair fight, but I made that fight. I was cocky and fast, and I got to wondering how fast I was. A man never finds out shooting at tin cans. I found out the only way there is." He stared over Chesbrough's shoulder. He had never talked to anyone like this before, but he wanted them to understand.

He said, "It was a bad thing," and the words sounded almost thoughtful. "It put me on the run. Not from the law, but from myself—and from other young kids who wanted the reputation I had. There's always somebody waiting who needs to prove something to himself." He thought, The traveling had been useless, for a man could never escape people or himself. He said roughly, "The law doesn't want you around, because where you are, trouble always crops up. Towns are afraid of you for the same reason."

He heard her say, "Oh," and for a moment, was afraid

to look at her. He did not want to see fear of him in her face. He turned his head and saw only pity in her eyes. It hit him hard. With her burden, she still could pity someone else.

He said flatly, "A man gets tired of running." There were all kinds of running, and the physical was the least. "Then he tries to pick a spot and stay."

Chesbrough's eyes flared with hope. Then the hope faded. "I can't pay you," he muttered.

Quade frowned at him. "I didn't hear any talk about pay. Can I put my horse in the barn?"

Chesbrough breathed a great sigh. "You sure can."

QUADE stepped out onto the porch, and she followed him. She looked squarely at him and asked, "How much talk did you hear in town?"

Her suffering was near the surface, and he did not blame her for being suspicious of him. The suspicion was a natural thing. A man heard talk, and she could assume he would ride out to see if there was anything in the talk to benefit him.

He said in a rough voice, "A person makes a mistake and lets it color everything he thinks and does. Anybody's a damn fool for carrying a mistake around with him." He was not fooling himself that it was as easy as the saying of it. The world worked hard to see that a person didn't forget a mistake.

He looked at her, and she was blinking against the tears in her eyes. "And if they won't let you forget?"

He thought her suspicions of him were gone. "Then make *them* forget it," he said roughly.

She said steadily, "Thank you, Mr. Quade."

The harshness of his tone increased. "You haven't got anything to thank me for. My being here can make it worse for you."

A small boy came around the corner of the house before she could speak. She looked at him, then back at Quade. "Did you know I had a son?"

"Sure," he said gruffly. "What's his name?"

"Jimmy," she answered.

He chuckled, and it was a pleasant sound, the more pleasant because it was totally unexpected in this harsh man. He said, "If that ain't the damnedest thing! My name's Jim."

She moved to him and placed her hand on his arm. Her voice was choked as she said, "I'm glad you're here."

He frowned at her, then looked at the litter in the yard. "We've got a lot of work to do around here."

He stood very still, afraid any movement would make her take her hand from his arm.

SIX

QUADE straightened and mopped his face with a bandanna. The midafternoon sun searched for the moisture in a man and sucked it out. But the pile of rubbish behind the house was growing to satisfying proportions. When he was through piling all the litter, he'd set a match to it. The land around the house was beginning to look orderly. The weeds in front of the porch needed a scythe taken to them, and Priam did not have one. It was only one of a dozen needed items. He needed hinges for sagging, scraping doors, nails for loose boards, and a decent hammer to drive them with.

Susan came out of the house, carrying a pail and a dipper. She handed him a dipperful of water and said, "It's cool. I just drew it."

He thanked her with the briefest of smiles. Something was happening, and he was afraid to examine it too closely. But in the space of a couple of days it was forming. He found himself listening for the sound of her steps, her voice. He had heard her laugh only once in that time, and he was anxious to hear it again.

She turned her head as the sound of Priam's singing came to them. He was hidden from them by the barn, and the singing was more enthusiastic than tuneful.

She said softly, "I wonder how long it's been since he's done that."

Quade soberly watched her. There was happiness in both her and Priam, if it were allowed to come out. He thought with a start of wonder, it's in me, too. But it had been encased in ice for so long that it was like a blade of spring grass, afraid to poke out lest a wintery blast wither it. His gun was in the barn with his bedroll. This was the longest waking period in years that he had not worn it.

Jimmy came around the corner of the house, his right hand tightly closed. He held out the hand and cautiously opened it.

51

"Quade," he said. "What's this?"

"Mr. Quade," his mother corrected.

Jimmy frowned at her, and Quade drawled, "Jimmy and I don't stand on any formalities." He knelt to examine the prize the boy held. It was easy to reach an understanding with a child. There was a lack of evasiveness in their natures grown-ups did not possess.

Jimmy held a beetle, its shell wonderfully colored, and the sun's ray struck a translucent sheen from it. Most grown-ups would have been too preoccupied to see it, but a boy had picked it up and found a moment's pleasure.

"What is it, Quade?" Jimmy repeated.

Quade could have made up a name, but he did not. He was going to have to learn more than he knew, if he wanted to answer a boy's questions.

"I don't know its name, Jimmy. It's a beetle of some kind."

Their heads were close together as they examined it. Jimmy looked at Quade, his face sober. "It's too pretty to kill."

The words hit Quade with a small shock. A child was too quickly touched by the grown-up world, for those words came directly out of it.

He said, "We're not going to kill it, Jimmy."

He lifted the insect from Jimmy's hand and set it on the ground. They watched it waddle away and hide under a leaf.

"Is that his home?" the boy asked.

"Right now, it is," Quade said gravely. He searched for words to tell the boy that the insect felt hidden and so felt secure. Every living creature needed that feeling. He was entangled in the thought, and he knew it would not come out right. He let it slip away.

He looked up, and her face was soft as she watched them.

His face fell into wooden lines again. That was his natural expression, and what was natural to a man was what he sought refuge in, even though it might not be the thing he wanted at all.

He said, "Run along now." He turned the boy and whacked him on the seat of the pants.

She waited until the boy turned the corner, then said,

"Mr. Quade,"—and stopped. He wished he knew the thoughts in her mind; he wished he knew clearly the ones in his.

To break the silence he said, "I need some things in town. Did you get everything you wanted the other day?"

He recognized the flicker of emotion in her eyes as a returning fear. The memory of the town did that to her, and he knew a quick hatred for it.

She said, "We need a lot of things. I bought only what we had to have. I'll make out a list." She drew a deep breath, and her head lifted. "No. I'll go with you."

He grunted, "Maybe that'd be better." He wanted to tell her how much he approved. After her experience with the town, that took courage. Maybe she felt he was a leaf, temporarily hiding her. A wry look came into his eyes at the thought.

"I'll hitch up the horses," he said and walked toward the barn.

He opened his bedroll and searched for his one clean shirt. He scowled as he did not see it. He went through his belongings again, trying to remember when he had worn the shirt.

She came up behind him and asked, "Are you looking for this?" She held out the freshly ironed shirt. She took the look on his face for censure, and she said in a small voice, "I was ironing some other things. Another shirt made no difference."

Her eyes went to the scar of the old bullet wound in his shoulder. The skin was drawn and puckered, and it had never lost that reddish-purple hue.

He did not want her looking at it, and he took the shirt from her. He said, "Thanks. You got enough to do without looking after my things." His tone sounded ungrateful, and he wanted it that way. A man in his position had no right to the thoughts that kept crowding into his head. "I'll be ready in a minute," he said and turned his back on her. He felt her presence for a long moment, then the feeling faded, and he knew she was gone.

He hitched up Priam's horse and drove the wagon to the front of the house. At Jimmy's disappointed look, "You can go next time."

Priam's eyes were concerned as he looked up at him. He said, "You're not wearing your gun. Ain't you liable to need it?"

Quade said, "No," and lifted the reins. Maybe not wearing the gun could keep him out of trouble. He hoped so. At least it was an open announcement to everyone that he wanted none. He did not speak or look at her as he drove away. He did not have to see nor hear her to know she was beside him. The tingly feeling along his skin told him that.

THEY drove a considerable distance before she said, "I miss trees most of all."

He clucked to the horse and said, "Trees are right nice." His tongue was a clumsy tool, and he cursed it. "It's pretty fair grazing country, though." Chesbrough would never be able to run a large number of head on his two sections. But he could make a living, if he were left alone. He could not make one, if he kept on finding one of his steers shot and another missing. Quade thought, maybe we can put a stop to that.

They rode the remainder of the distance in silence. The town was in sight, when she said, "Quade, why are people so cruel?"

He shook his head. "I dunno. The funny part of it is that they don't think they are. They'd be plumb upset if you accused them of it."

She said in a low dark voice, "Sometimes I hate people."

He sympathized with the way she felt, but the feeling did no good. It never hurt the people. He said dryly, "It's hard to live without them."

He drove down the street, and he was aware she sat stiffly beside him, looking straight ahead. She's a tough one, he thought admiringly. Give her a little support, and she'll whip this town.

He stopped in front of the general store and said, "I've got to go to the hardware store. You be all right?"

She said, "Yes." Her lips were tightly compressed in anxiety.

A fat woman came down the walk, stopped for a moment, and put malignant eyes upon Susan. The eyes went from Susan to Quade, and he felt as though he had been clawed. The woman sniffed, tossed her head, and continued down the walk.

He wanted to break the stricken look on Susan's face, and he drawled, "I take it that she's no friend of ours."

She would not look at him, and color was high in her cheeks. "That was Mrs. Wilson." He had to lean toward her to catch her voice. "She used to know me—" he thought her voice was going to falter before she could finish—"some time ago."

It told him a good deal; it told him that much of her unhappiness here lay in the fat woman. Righteous women were hell. They could hurt someone with the natural vindictiveness of a bobcat.

He said sharply, "You want me to go in with you?"

She met his eyes, and he knew the suffering in them. "No, I'm all right," she said and moved up the steps.

He shook his head half admiringly and half compassionately before he crossed the street. Two customers were in the hardware store when he entered, and their talk stopped. He was aware of their covert glances, while he hefted one scythe after another. These glances irritated him, and he knew how much torture they must be to a woman. A woman was more thin-skinned than a man.

He bought the scythe, three pairs of hinges, a hammer, and ten pounds of nails. He thought the total cost of his purchases was high, but he would not quibble about it— not this time. The storekeeper was relieved when Quade paid the bill and gathered up his items. He was in here unarmed, and seeking no trouble, and still he was not wanted.

He shouldered the scythe, picked up his other things, and walked to the door. An icy gleam was in his eyes. Priam had known this feeling for some time. They might not want him around, but they took his money gladly enough.

He stowed the scythe and the other articles in the back of the wagon and leaned against it, waiting for Susan to finish her shopping. He looked down the street, and Osley and Hobart were coming toward him. His straightening was a casual movement, and only the narrowing of his eyes told of the mounting tension within him.

Osley stopped before him and frowned. He said uncertainly, "I thought you said you were leaving."

Quade caught the weak note of complaint in his voice. "Changed my mind," Quade said. Hobart's eyes were fastened on him. The man's hunger was written all over his face.

Osley said, "Quade, I told you I didn't want any trouble around here."

Quade said mildly, "I'm not looking for any." He pointed out the obvious. "I'm not wearing a gun."

Hobart said slyly, "Maybe you feel safer that way."

Quade put cold eyes on him. Some men were never content unless they were constantly prodding at things. He could not put too much censure in the thought—once, *he* had prodded.

Susan came out of the store, and Quade cursed the unfortunate timing.

Hobart's eyes went to her, then back to Quade. "I was wondering what changed your mind," he said with a nasty edge. "It sure ain't hard to see the reason for it now."

Quade prayed she was not close enough to hear Hobart. He took a long step, and his fist was swinging at the completion of it. It gave him the maximum leverage of movement and body. He smashed Hobart in the mouth, and the man went reeling backwards. His foot turned under him at the edge of the walk, and he fell on his back. Dust puffed up from under his shoulders, and his head rolled back and forth in a dazed motion. Blood spurted from his split lip, covering his chin and staining his shirt.

"Get up," Quade said. "Get up."

Hobart shook his head, trying to clear the swimming in his eyes. He came up to a knee, his movements poorly coordinated. He wiped the back of his hand across his bloody mouth and stared at it for a long moment, and Osley knew him better than Quade did, for he guessed at the thoughts whipping through Hobart's mind before Quade saw any indication of it. Osley jumped across the walk with surprising speed for his bulk. His boot was swinging just as Hobart's hand moved toward his gun.

"Stobie," he yelled. The boot hit the hand as it touched the gunbutt. He kicked it away from the gun and yelled, "That's murder, Stobie. He's unarmed."

Hobart looked from Quade to Osley, and the hatred spilling out of his eyes included both of them with its intensity.

Osley jerked him to his feet, and turned and shoved him down the street. "Get out of here until you cool off," he ordered. "You started this. Don't be blaming anyone but yourself."

Hobart took a few steps, then looked back at Quade. "I'm not forgetting this, Quade."

"That makes two of us," Quade answered savagely.

"Go on, Stobie," Osley shouted. His tone had the bite of authority, and Hobart moved away.

Osley looked at Quade and said heavily, "I gotta say this wasn't your fault. Stobie had to mouth off—" He shook his head and did not finish the sentence. His face was gloomy as he said, "But things like this will keep happening as long as you're around."

Quade shrugged. He felt more respect for Osley than he knew a few days ago. Osley had judged this matter fairly and impartially.

He said in a level voice, "I'm coming into town whenever I need to. I won't wear a gun, and I'll promise you nothing more."

His words brought no relief to Osley's face. "I can't keep you out," Osley muttered. He looked at Susan and shook his head. "Stobie ain't the only one who will be picking at you." He moved away, his shoulders bent. He looked like a man foreseeing a busy and disagreeable future.

Quade looked at Susan. She seemed frozen motionless on the porch. He went up the steps and took the packages from her arms. "Finished?" he asked her gently.

She mutely nodded, and he placed her purchases in the wagon. He helped her into it, and she did not speak until they were quite a way out of town.

"How did it start?" she asked in a faint voice.

"Just an argument," he said brusquely.

He thought tears were very near the surface from the

way her voice shook. "It was about me, wasn't it?" she asked.

"Damn it," he said harshly. "It was a personal argument."

She was not convinced, but at least, the tears didn't spill over.

SEVEN

COLONEL MACLENDON strode into the bunkhouse and looked at his crew of four men. The laughter and banter stopped immediately upon his entrance, and each man stirred uneasily, as though he thought the full force of the colonel's attention was on him. Each of them had the thought, what did I do wrong today? The colonel was a hard man, and he tolerated few mistakes.

MacLendon said in that cold, composed voice, "I guess all of you know that Chesbrough has hired a known killer."

Ellis excitedly bobbed his head. He was a short balding man and the end of a day's work rested more heavily upon him than it used to do. His legs were bent, and the right one dragged when he walked. His horny hands were-rope and leather-scarred, and his face was crosshatched from scouring winds and merciless suns. His eagerness to please was plainly discernible—add a few more years toll to the price already extracted from him, and who would have him? As hard a man as the colonel was, Ellis wanted to stay on here. It was in his voice and manner.

He said, "You mean Jim Quade, Colonel?" An unconscious fawning was in his tone, and he would have been outraged toward anyone pointing it out. He didn't wait for the colonel's nod before he continued, "I saw him go up against the three Downey brothers in Abilene. Tom Smith was plumb sore about it, but the Downeys jumped Quade. All Smith could do was to tell Quade to get out of town." Ellis added dubiously. "I never seen anyone as fast as this Quade. He killed two of the Downeys and crippled the other."

MacLendon's cold eyes bored into him. "Ellis, you know so damned much about Quade, you'll be a good man for the job I have in mind for tomorrow."

Ellis's eyes were agonized, but he dared not protest.

"You'll need help," MacLendon said. His eyes rested in turn on each of the three. "I'm tired of fooling around with Chesbrough. If he wants to make a fight of it, he'll get one. I'm going to run him and his hired gunman off. Hartack, you go with Ellis tomorrow."

"What's the job?" Hartack asked suspiciously. His youth made him brash, even with the colonel. But the road stretched broad and long before him; it wasn't narrow and pinched as it was for Ellis. If Hartack did not work for the colonel, there were other jobs. It was a simple matter to saddle up and ride to them.

"You're going to dynamite Chesbrough's spring," Mac-Lendon said. He hated the decision, for he had wanted that spring. But Quade's coming changed the picture. Now it was best to get this over with as quickly as possible. He recalled how Jonse had momentarily faced Quade, and the fear stirred again. If Quade stayed around here, Jonse could face him again, and there might be no one to stop him. "That will drive him out faster than anything I know."

Ellis sucked in his breath in a small sound of protest. He asked weakly, "Just the two of us?"

"Just the two of you."

Fear and worry made Ellis reckless. "It'd be better if more of us went."

"It wouldn't be better," MacLendon snapped. "Four men are easier to see than two. Keep out of Quade's sight, if that's what's worrying you."

The worried gnawing drove Ellis to overlook the warning in MacLendon's tone. "Why don't Wilkie and Jonse go with us? With four of us, Quade might be scared—"

MacLendon took two strides toward him. He hit him at the completion of the second one. The blow lifted Ellis off his feet and knocked him against a wall. He slid down it and landed on his shoulders. He looked at MacLendon with dazed eyes, feebly wiping at the blood that leaked from his mouth.

"You can draw your pay," MacLendon said.

"No, Colonel," Ellis said in agonized entreaty. "I wasn't raising no objection. I'll go."

"That's better," MacLendon said. He swung his eyes to Hartack. "Anything you want to say?" he asked softly.

Hartack looked at Ellis with sullen eyes. He looked back at MacLendon and shrugged. "I got no objections," he said.

"Good." MacLendon stepped to the door.

The silence held for a long time after MacLendon left. Hartack smashed his fist into his palm. He looked at Ellis and said savagely, "God damn it. God damn it, anyhow."

One of the two other men asked softly, "You raising your objections now, Hartack? Ain't you a mite late?"

Hartack fluently cursed him, and Simmons grinned with malicious enjoyment.

QUADE stepped down from the saddle and approached the spring. There was a shining reverence in his eyes as he gazed at one nature's bountiful blessings. In this land of sparse water, a man was indeed fortunate to own such a source of water. He stretched out full length and dipped his lips into the pool of water. The water was sweet and cool, and he knew it came from deep within the earth's bowels. He stood up and wiped his lips with the back of his hand. "You're a lucky man," he said.

"It's really something," Chesbrough said, pride undisguised in his voice. "I don't know how many thousands of gallons it flows in a day."

Quade's eyes followed the course of the water. From the pool it ran downhill into a much larger basin near the foot of the hill. The upper part of the spring was fenced off, but the basin would water all the cattle Chesbrough could ever possibly run. The water still had enough strength after filling the basin to run a fair-sized stream for two or three hundred yards before the thirsty soil absorbed it.

Quade asked, "Is this your only source of water?"

Chesbrough waved his hand to his right. "There's a couple of wet-weather springs over there. And the crick runs a couple of months a year. But this is the only water I have that's permanent. Oldtimers tell me this spring has never been known to go dry."

Quade's face was reflective. This spring alone made Priam's land highly valuable. He asked, "MacLendon ever use this water?"

"He used it while I was gone. I've got some bad wire between him and me. It's old and rotten. A cow leans against it for a mouthful of grass on the other side, and she falls through it. Some of his cattle still drift over this way. I wouldn't mind him using the water," he said earnestly. "But I ain't got enough graze for his cattle and mine. I tried to explain that to him."

Quade grunted. MacLendon was a cattleman; he didn't need that explanation.

Priam said. "I been aiming to put up a new fence between him and me, but one thing or another happened, and I never got around to it." He looked squarely at Quade, and a wry grin moved his lips. "To tell the truth, I was afraid to build it. I'd like to get started on it now."

"That's next on the list," Quade said absently. His eyes were fixed on the water. Priam was terribly vulnerable here. If anything happened to this spring, the land would be almost worthless to him.

He said, "I'm surprised MacLendon hasn't hit this spring before now."

Priam shook his head. "He wouldn't harm it. He's still hoping to get it."

Quade tried to look at this through MacLendon's eyes. Before Quade came, MacLendon had been content with petty annoyances and abuse against Priam Chesbrough. Perhaps he had enjoyed dragging it out. But now conditions were changed. Quade's presence made the old tactics dangerous. MacLendon should attempt a more serious blow, one heavy enough to end it fast.

He said, "If it was me, I'd settle down to break you. I'd start by dynamiting this spring."

Priam's eyes went round with alarm. "He wouldn't do that!"

Quade said caustically, "Don't bet on it." He had no wish to scare Priam, but a feeling was gnawing away at him, a feeling he could not put into words. It had happened before, and rarely was the feeling wrong. A man never lost anything by putting a little extra caution on the weak spots, and this looked like one to him.

He moved back to his horse and mounted. He looked back at the spring as they rode away. A man could only judge another's possible action by what he himself would do. If he were MacLendon, he would hit the spring.

He WAS preoccupied during supper, and Susan noticed it. He moved outside after the meal and sat on the porch, smoking and moodily staring in the direction of the spring. She came out and joined him, and several minutes went by before she spoke. It was hard to concentrate on his thinking, with her here.

She asked, "What's troubling you, Mr. Quade?"

It hit him with a small jolt that she never called him by his first name, and he wondered why. "Nothing," he said irritably. In the following silence, he thought she was probably offended, and his irritation grew. He had enough on his mind without adding additional worry.

She said softly, "All right, Jim," and lightly touched his arm before she left.

He grinned a little foolishly. Women seemed to have an instinct for reading a man's mind. He went back to his original thinking and muttered to himself, "Mac-Lendon, you won't run them off."

If he were going to hit the spring, what hours would he pick? Not the major portion of the daylight ones; the night hours were good, but he tried to narrow it even more. Between midnight and dawn were the hours he would pick. A man's alertness was more likely to be buried deep under heavy sleep. He might stand a chance at picking the hours, but the night would be left entirely to chance. It could be tonight, or the next, or a week from now. He growled at the thought of sleepless hours ahead to be spent on that hill.

He snapped his unfinished cigarette away and got to his feet. He walked toward the barn. He could get a few hours' sleep before midnight.

He looked back toward the house, and the light behind her silhouetted Susan in the doorway. He lifted his hand in acknowledgment and saw her wave in return.

Sleep did not come as readily at he wished. The moonlight filtered in through the cracks in the barn, and he twisted and turned. A great restlessness seized him, and all kinds of thoughts crowded into his mind. It was during the hours a man spent with himself that the loneliness really swept in, and he wondered if there would ever be an end to it. He could still see her standing in that doorway, and the loneliness beat at him. He wondered if she— He abruptly clamped down upon that line of thinking. A man was a fool to try to delve too far into the future. He could live only a day at a time, and he might as well accept it that way. . . .

He slept some before midnight. He came awake, and judging from the passage of the moon, he was not too

far off from the time he wanted to be going. He kicked
the air out of Wrangle's belly and cinched the saddle.
Wrangle snorted lugubriously at this nocturnal work.
Quade slid the carbine into its saddle scabbard and
pulled on the reins. Wrangle did not want to leave the
barn, and Quade had to drag him out. He mounted, and
looked at the dark house before he moved the horse on
its way. He was tying a lot of his life to those people,
and he knew why, but he would not let her name form
in his mind. A man paid a price for everything he got
in this life—either in work, or time, or money. Maybe
he was whittling away at the price by doing this.

He left Wrangle half a mile from the spring and hoped
it was far enough away that the horse would not bugle
to any approaching riders.

While the moon gave some light, it was not strong
enough to see small objects clearly. He cursed once as a
rock turned under his foot. He changed the carbine to
the crook of his left arm and went on, his eyes intent
on the ground. The night was warm, and there was one
thing he did not want to run across—a damned rattle-
snake. He hated those things.

He climbed the hill on the opposite side of the spring
and found as comfortable a spot as possible. He was
nearly a hundred yards above it, and in daylight this
position would give him a wide sweep of the country.
He dozed intermittently, coming awake each time with a
start. This could readily be a fool's errand, but a man
went on a lot of those during a lifetime. Toward morning, it grew a little chilly, and he could feel its sly fingers
digging deeper into his flesh. He shifted his position to
ease his cramped mucles, grunting as he did so. There
was no other complaint; he had known many such nights
as this.

BLACK changed to gray in the eastern sky, then a tiny
line of rosy hue appeared, pushing a blue band ahead
of it. This would be the hour he would pick, but it looked
as though he were wrong on the day.

He said a soft *ah* as two dots appeared in the dim
light—close together, and moving this way. He peered
as them with an intensity that distorted his vision and
made his eyes swim, and he looked away for a moment.
When he refocused his eyes, the dots were close enough

to identify as horsemen. He stretched out on his belly, the carbine held loosely in his right hand. The waiting was almost over.

He did not move in the ensuing twenty minutes, and he was aware of no stress. The two riders left their horses at the foot of the hill and climbed toward the spring. The taller one carried a package of some kind. Quade could stop them now, but still he waited. Honest riders were rarely about at this hour, but it was possible they merely wanted a drink. He grinned cynically at the thought. But it would hurt nothing to wait for a little more proof of their intentions.

Their voices carried to him as they climbed, but he could not make out the words. Then the taller man's words sharpened and became distinct. "See, Ellis," the man said. "You been fretting all this way for no reason at all."

"We ain't through yet," Ellis grumbled. "Let's get it over with."

They were directly below him, and the light was now much stronger. Ellis carried a short-handled shovel, and he dug a hole at the mouth of the spring. He put down the shovel and took the package from the other man's hands. He pulled half a dozen sticks of dynamite out of a brown paper bag and tied them into a bundle. Quade snugged the carbine butt to his shoulder as Ellis capped the middle stick. He watched him fuse the bundle, place it in the hole, then tamp the dirt around it. His eyes were bright, and his breathing was slow and even.

The taller man seemed bored with the entire process, for he repeatedly yawned. A cold smile was on Quade's face as he speculated on how quickly the yawn would disappear if the man knew what was above him.

Ellis played out a hundred feet of fuse, and the expression on his face was intently concentrated. Quade's finger slipped inside the trigger guard as Ellis pulled out a match. He let him wipe the match on an upraised pants leg and saw it spring into life before he pulled the trigger.

The carbine's spiteful crack came with shocking unexpectedness to the two men below. Ellis uttered a wild cry, and one of his arms flung wide, while he grabbed at his shoulder with the other hand. He staggered and lost his footing. He went down hard, jolting another cry from him. He rolled a dozen yards before he managed to stop.

The taller man clapped a hand to his gunbutt, and Quade yelled, "Do you want your damned head blown off?"

The man's hand fell away from the gun, and Quade said, "Unbuckle that belt and step away from it."

The man remained motionless a long moment as though he were hanging on the thin edge of a decision. Quade rose into view, the carbine still at his shoulder.

"Don't, Hartack," Ellis yelled. "It's Quade." His voice sounded almost tearful. "Damn it," he moaned. "I told the colonel."

Hartack's face was red with anger and frustration. He said, "You son of a bitch," but his fingers fumbled the buckle open, and he stepped away from the dropped gunbelt.

Quade came down the hill, the carbine ready at his waist, though he doubted there was any danger in either of them. Ellis still wore his gun, but using it was the farthest thing from his mind as he clutched his right shoulder and moaned. Quade suspected the shoulder was shattered. A carbine slug could drill clean or smash bone with equal effect. Ellis's shoulder looked sort of caved in.

Keeping part of his attention on Hartack, Quade leaned down and jerked the gun from Ellis's holster. He threw it far down the hill, then faced Hartack. The man's eyes were hot with fury.

Quade stopped a couple of feet from him. He said almost pleasantly, "You've got a fat mouth." His hands moved with startling speed, and the carbine butt swung upward from his waist. Hartack made a frightened squawk. He tried to fall back and throw up his arms at the same time. Neither move was effective. The butt smashed through the weak defense of his arms and crashed against his jaw. Quade did not put full force into the blow. He used it as a warning, not to knock out the man. It split skin along Hartack's jaw and smashed him back. He staggered and went down to a knee. He held his hand to his bleeding chin and looked at Quade with dazed and swimming eyes.

Ellis's eyes were round with terror, and momentarily he forgot his pain. "You going to kill us?" he whimpered.

Quade's eyes held no compassion. "I will, if I ever catch you around here again." He turned his head toward Hartack. "Help him to his horse. And tell MacLendon that if that spring is ever bothered I'll come straight to him."

Hartack looked as though he had something to say, but he looked at Quade's face and wisely held it. He got to his feet and shook his head. Drops of blood flew at the movement. He helped Ellis to his feet, and Ellis screamed with pain. "My God, it hurts," he whimpered. He tried to move the arm and bit his lip. "It's broke bad," he said to Hartack. For the first time the realization of the future hit him hard. "My God," he said. "Maybe I'll never be able to work again. Damn you, Quade," he said fiercely. "Why didn't you kill me?"

Hartack growled, "Come on," and led him down the hill. He helped Ellis into the saddle, and his help was not particularly gentle. He rode off, leaving Ellis to follow as best as he could.

Quade turned and kicked out the dynamite. He pulled the fuse loose and carefully detached the cap. He coiled the fuse and hung it over a shoulder. It was still an hour to breakfast. He was hungry as hell.

Priam was in the barn when Quade rode in. He said, "I've been waiting out here for an hour. I was afraid you'd—" He hesitated, then said honestly, "Left."

Quade growled, "My bedroll's still here."

Priam's eyes widened as he saw the dynamite under Quade's arm and the coil of fuse over his shoulder. "What are you doing with dynamite?" he asked.

Quade dismounted and put the explosive on a shelf. He stripped saddle and bridle off of Wrangle before he answered. He debated telling Chesbrough what had happened, knowing the worry it would cause him. But Chesbrough was a man, and he'd have to face everything that came along.

He said, "MacLendon sent it over. Without his compliments."

Priam's face blanched. "He was after the spring?" he whispered.

Quade nodded. "Sent two men. MacLendon won't like their report." What MacLendon did about the report depended upon how hard the man was. Quade doubted

MacLendon would ride in open force against them—at least, not for a while. That was usually the last resort, and Quade thought MacLendon would try some other devious device first. He was sure MacLendon would try something. He wanted to take the apprehension out of Priam's eyes, and he said, "Maybe he'll let us alone for a while, Priam."

Priam drew a deep breath. "Damn him," he said. His expression changed, though there was still concern in it. "Maybe we ought not to tell Susan about it. She'd only worry."

Quade nodded. A man should have to face up to things—and he should try to shield a woman all he possibly could from doing the same.

He heard Susan's call from the back door.

"That's breakfast," Priam said.

"I'm ready for it," Quade answered.

He sat down to a breakfast of hotcakes, fried ham and potatoes. The hotcakes kept a man eating long after he should have stopped.

She put the fourth stack of cakes on his plate, and Jimmy looked at it and said, "Quade, you sure eat a lot."

"Jimmy!" his mother said in a reproving voice, but her lip corners were twitching.

Quade said gravely, "It's not my fault. It's because the cooking's so good." He looked at Susan, and her eyes were bright over the color in her cheeks. She met his eyes for a long moment before she turned back to the stove.

He could not finish the fourth stack. He groaned, "Susan, I can't." He shoved back from the table and stood. "If I keep on eating like this, I'll wind up with a bel—" He glanced at Jimmy. "I mean a stomach as big as a cow."

"Quade, is a stomach the same as a belly?" Jimmy asked.

Susan covered her face with her apron, and Quade shook his head at the boy. "You hear too much." He rumpled Jimmy's hair and walked to the door. He felt good, and it sprang from a deep contentment, something he had not known for a long time.

He strolled out into the yard, and Priam followed

him. He said, "Quade, I'm going to sell enough head to buy the wire we need to put that fence in."

"Good," Quade said absently. He kept glancing in the direction of town as Priam rattled on. Priam expected more approval, and he said testily, "You ain't heard anything I've said." A thought struck him, and his face tightened. "You're expecting someone," he accused. His voice unconsciously dropped a notch. "The MacLendons?"

"I doubt it," Quade answered. Maybe he was wrong in expecting anyone. He said, "Let's go fix that toolshed."

The south wall of the small structure had known too much exposure to weather. Dry rot had started in the nail holes and spread. The boards still hung on the nails, but any stiff breeze would rattle them. Other boards were cracked and warped. Quade pried them off with a bar, and Priam stacked them. They were fit for kindling for the cooking stove and nothing more.

Osley found them there. He said in a troubled voice, "Quade, I've got a complaint against you."

Quade laid down his pinch-bar and mopped his face. His shirt was sodden with sweat and clinging to his back. He was uncomfortable and relatively short-tempered. "Go on," he snapped.

"Colonel MacLendon claims you shot one of his men."

"I did." Quade's hard eyes never left Osley's face.

Osley's eyes went startled. He had not expected so ready an admision. "Just because they were crossing Chesbrough's land?"

"Because they were sent to dynamite Chesbrough's spring." Quade saw disbelief in Osley's face and said harshly, "You come with me."

He led Osley into the barn and placed the bundle of dynamite and the coiled fuse in his hands. "If that's not enough I can show you the hole they dug for this. I can show you where Ellis bled."

Uncertainty twisted Osley's face. He had ridden out here with a set mind, and he did not want to admit facts that might change it.

"Did you talk to Ellis?" Quade demanded.

Osley slowly shook his head. "MacLendon said I could see him later. He claimed he was at the doctor's."

"You won't see him," Quade said. "I'm betting Mac-

Lendon has already sent him on his way. I shattered his shoulder. He won't be able to work for a long time. He'll be useless to MacLendon. MacLendon won't keep him around—he's that kind."

He stared hard at Osley and asked, "You still ready to call me a liar?"

Osley muttered, "No." He had come out here without knowing all there was to know about this. A note of complaint crept into his voice. "You told me you wouldn't wear a gun."

"I said I wouldn't wear one in town. There's a difference."

He watched the edges of the set convictions in Osley's mind crumble. He said, "You might as well know it. I've kind of taken over this place. Anybody rides against it rides against me."

Osley's face was heavy. He started out of the barn and said sorrowfully, "There's going to be trouble ahead."

"I expect so," Quade said dryly. He felt just a little more tolerant toward Osley. Osley might be weak, but his mind was not completely closed.

EIGHT

QUADE and Priam combed the two sections of land, and when they finished there were sixteen head of steers and two old cows that would never calve again in the corral. Quade shook his head as he looked at the handful of animals. It was a hell of a small drive.

"Is that all?" he asked.

Priam said doubtfully, "I thought I had five more steers."

Quade sharply glanced at him. The doubt in Priam's voice was not for the five steers—he knew he'd had them.

Quade said, "We'll go look for them." When a man had this small a number to sell, he needed every additional head he could get. Even then, it was not going to bring any startling amount of money. These animals were a poor lot, all of them showing too much leg. A man could have ridden horseback under a couple of them without knocking off his hat. Priam needed his stock upgraded.

"We beat it pretty thoroughly," Priam objected. "Even if they'd been down, we'd seen some sign of them."

"I didn't mean to look here for them," Quade said. "With all that bad wire, they could easily be on MacLendon's land."

Priam's face was quite still. "I wouldn't want to start anything for five head."

Quade said, "They belong to you, don't they?"

Priam reluctantly nodded.

"Would you know them?"

"I'd know them, all right. Two of them were brockfaced. One was a roan—"

Quade interrupted, "Then let's go get them."

Priam took a long breath, and his mouth firmed. He said quietly, "They belong to me, and I want them."

Quade glanced at him as they rode. There was probably fear nibbling at his thoughts, but it did not show on his face. He thought with satisfaction, he's come back up the road a long way.

They found wire down on the northeast corner of Priam's land, and half a mile over on MacLendon's land they saw a herd of cattle grazing.

Quade grunted, "Maybe those five head are with that bunch." If so, it would be easier than he hoped.

As they approached the cattle Priam said, "I see two of them." He stood up in his stirrups, and relief was in his face. "There's the others. They're all here." His thoughts showed on his face. With luck, they could cut out the five head and be off MacLendon's land before anyone saw them.

Quade said, "You hold. I'll cut." Wrangle was good at it. He seemed to guess a cow's intention of turning before the animal even knew it. Quade had a minimum of trouble with four of them, but the fifth, the roan steer, was a different matter. He did not want to leave the herd, and he kept ducking into it.

Quade swore. The herd was getting restless, and he did not want to rile it into running. He rode along side the steer and lashed at its head with the coils of his rope. The steer blatted and whirled to his right. Quade beat at him again, and Wrangle kept in tight against the animal, forcing him away from the herd. The steer made one more attempt, then gave up. There was no escaping this horse that stuck to him like a burr, and he moved decilely enough in the direction the horse wanted him to go.

Quade drove him toward the four Priam was holding, and he saw the tightening in Priam's face before Priam spoke. He pulled up, and Priam said, "They're coming, Quade."

Quade looked around and saw three horsemen. The distance was a little far to be sure, but it looked like MacLendon and his two sons.

He said, "Drive them on back, Priam. I'll wait for them."

He saw the refusal forming in Priam's face and said harshly, "I can handle it." If it came to guns, Priam wouldn't be much help, and there were Susan and the boy to think of. No man could predict how a gunfight would come out, and Quade did not want them left alone.

He sat Wrangle with indolent ease while he waited for them. None of his tenseness showed in his face, but he didn't like this. He was on MacLendon's land, and there were three of them.

The three pulled up thirty feet from him, and Mac-Lendon said coldly, "What are you doing here?"

Quade said in a mild voice, "Came after some steers that strayed." He jerked his thumb over his shoulder. "Priam's driving them home now."

Jonse leaned forward and said challengingly, "How do we know they belong to him?"

Wilkie's face was sullen, and he would not directly look at Quade.

Quade put most of his attention on the other two. Jonse was a hothead and would force this all the way. As yet, he did not know the full measurement of MacLendon. He did not entirely discount Wilkie. Wilkie would probably join in any action either of the other two started.

He said, "The man says they belong to him." His tone roughened. "I believe him." His hand moved nearer his gunbutt. He glanced at MacLendon, then put the full force of his eyes upon Jonse. The implication was plain. He expected Jonse to start this, and he would go after Jonse first.

MacLendon's face went pinched. The three of them might get Quade, but it was a certainty that he would take at least one of them; and the first one would be Jonse. Quade's unwavering attention said so. He said, "Jonse," in sharp warning and pulled Jonse's look toward him. "They belong to Chesbrough," he said crisply. "I saw them with our stuff the other day."

Quade let a slow sigh slip from him. MacLendon was avoiding a showdown because of his fear for Jonse.

Jonse said hotly, "You're not going to let him get away with this!"

MacLendon's eyes blazed at him. "That's enough," he ordered. "I'd be ashamed to lay claim to those animals." He looked at Quade and saved a little face. "I'll let it pass this time. But I'm warning you, the next time I see you on my land, I'll shoot on sight."

Quade said dryly, "That's fair enough." He had sent the same warning to MacLendon a couple of mornings ago.

He sat his horse and watched them ride away. Jonse was boiling under his father's restraint. It showed in the stiff lines of his back. Quade wiped the back of his hand across his brow, and there was a little moisture on it. That had been tight. Quade would not risk a next time. That damned fence had to be fixed. He whirled Wrangle and spurred after Priam and the steers.

T HEY drove the cattle into town, and the buyer looked them over, dubiously shaking his head. He said, "Five dollars a round." His tone sounded final.

Acceptance was in Priam's face, and Quade said, "Six." He made the figure cold and final. He was pushing the man hard, and he would settle for five-fifty.

The cattle buyer pursed his lips and grumbled, "You drive a hard deal. I'll lose money on every head. Damn it, man. I can't do it."

Quade let him talk. Usually when a man talked on and on instead of giving a flat no, he was weakening. He sat staring at the man, and the buyer said, "All right. Six. But I'm losing money. You owe me a drink, at least."

Quade grinned. "I'll buy that drink." He felt pretty good as he watched the buyer count money into Priam's hand.

Priam was elated as they rode away from town. He said, "I'll come in after the wire in the morning. Quade, I can't say enough thanks."

"You don't owe me any thanks," Quade said gruffly. "You raised those head."

He knew Priam felt good, too. A little money in a man's pockets, money he earned himself, always gave a man that feeling. . . .

It took a week of hard work to run the fence. A lot of the proceeds of Priam's sale of his steers went into that new wire. Building fence was a hard, monotonous job. A man walked miles, first, in settling the posts, and they had had to replace a lot of the rotten posts in this line. Then, he walked some more in laying out the wire, and after the stretcher was on it, he walked some more, seeing that the wire did not bind or drag in any spot.

Quade drove the last staple and straightened. Three strands of wire stretched gleaming bright. He plucked at one of the wires, and it hummed with a pleasant tightness.

He said, "That's done, Priam." He grinned and said, "How'd you like to do this for a living?"

Priam groaned and flexed his hands. "Those damned holes. Why did the good Lord have to put rock so near the surface?"

Quade chuckled. Some of those post holes had been pure murder. They were able to drive a good number of the posts, but for the others, rock had to be laboriously pounded and barred from the holes.

Priam asked hopefully, "It will keep down trouble, won't it, Quade?"

"Maybe," Quade answered laconically. He doubted it. Priam did too, or he would not have voiced the question. The new fence would keep Priam's cattle from straying, if it were allowed to remain. Its remaining was the question. It was odd how new wire could be such an affront to men. They might pass old wire day after day hardly noticing it, but new wire was different; it stands out in sharp contrast to its surroundings.

He started gathering up the tools and putting them into the wagon. His shoulders ached, and soreness cramped his hands. Several angry scratches showed on his arms above the leather gloves. He never could handle barbed wire without its nicking him. He put a final glance on the fence before he drove away. Until that fence was an accepted fact by all parties concerned, it was going to demand a good deal of his attention.

HARTACK knocked on the door of the big house. He knocked rather gently, as though afraid to disturb anyone inside.

MacLendon came to the door, and Hartack said, "Colonel, they finished the fence this morning."

MacLendon's eyes burned. "Do the damned fools think I'll let it stand?" He had not minded the old wire; he could cross it almost anywhere he pleased. But this new wire was different. It was a symbol of Chesbrough's new resistance, digging in as though he expected to stay. The thought built a wildness in him, and he glared at Hartack.

Hartack stirred uneasily. He wished he had let one of the others bring this news.

"Are you afraid of Quade?" MacLendon snapped.

"I owe that bastard something," Hartack said viciously.

"Good," MacLendon said. The contempt was thinly veiled in his eyes. This young fool didn't have enough sense to be afraid. "Take Simmons and Wesley with you. I want that fence cut in a thousand places. There's fifty dollars extra for you when you get back."

Hartack's eyes gleamed. That fifty dollars meant several additional nights of pleasure with Tilda at the Orient Saloon. Tilda was expensive—she expected a man to spend money on her.

He said, "I'll wreck that damned fence, Colonel," and swaggered away. He really didn't have a lot to worry about. Quade was only a man; Chesbrough didn't count at all. Look how many times he had proven himself a coward. That left only Quade, and what could a lone man do against three of them?

Jonse came to the door as MacLendon turned away from it. "I heard that," he said. "I want in on that little party."

"You'll stay here," MacLendon snapped. He might have let Wilkie go, but not Jonse. Much of Quade's reputation could have been built by legend, but there had to be enough solid basis to get the reputation started. MacLendon remembered how Quade had stared at Jonse, and fear was a little shiver rippling along his skin. He would not let Jonse go against any part of that reputation—not when he could hire men like Hartack and the others for a few dollars.

He asked, "Where's Wilkie?"

"Sleeping," Jonse said in disgruntled tones. He was bored too much of the time. That fence-wrecking party would have been a welcome diversion.

"Was he drunk again last night?"

Jonse grinned. "If he wasn't, he was giving a damned good imitation of it."

MacLendon swore and strode toward the door of the bedroom.

Jonse laughed. Wilkie was in for a rude awakening.

QUADE put down his glasses and said, "They're coming."

"How many?" That was a breathless note in Priam's voice.

"Three." Quade put a quick glance on Priam's face.

Was the old fear of the MacLendons seizing him again?

"God damn them," Priam said savagely.

Quade was satisfied. A fearful man could curse, but it would have a different, a weaker ring to it. He looked through the glasses again, studying the approaching riders. He said, "We'll go on foot."

Priam uttered a quick objection. "That'll take us too long."

Quade nodded. Priam was right. And while that time was being consumed, damage would be done the fence. He said, "If we ride, they'll pick us up almost as soon as we start." Then the three men would either make a fight of it or they would run; Quade proposed to block both those actions.

He looked through the glasses again and saw the three reach the fence. One of them dismounted, and Quade waited until he was sure of the direction the man was working. He could not see the wire going down, but he was certain it was, and anger vibrated in his temples.

The man was working north, and Quade picked his course. There was a patch of brush several hundred yards ahead of the man and within pistol range of the fence. A shallow draw started at the brush's edge and deepened after seventy-five or a hundred yards. If the three were absorbed enough in their work, even the shallow part of the draw would afford enough conceal-ment to reach the brush. The two horsemen moved with the man on foot, one of them leading the riderless horse. Quade judged the pace of the work against the time he thought it would take to reach the patch of brush. It would be cutting it thin, but he thought they could make it. He could shoot at them from a much greater distance away and drive them off, but he wanted to catch them in the midst of their work; he wanted to send them back with something to remember. He handled Priam the carbine and said tersely, "Let's go." He evalu-ated the eagerness in Priam's face; he would have to keep that eagerness under control. . . .

Forty posts of cut wire were behind Hartack, and he had enjoyed every snip of the pliers. But the enjoyment was wearing thin. He was getting tired of walking, and he was bleeding from a cut on his right wrist where a wire had twanged back after its cutting, its barb biting deep.

He sucked on the cut and said, "Wesley, get down here and do some work." He swore at Wesley's uneasy expression and said, "Hell, there's no one within miles of us."

Wesley swung down and took the pliers from Hartack. "How much of this damned fence are we going to cut?"

"All of it," Hartack answered. He was thinking of the fifty dollars the colonel promised him. The colonel was going to get a job.

Simmons handed him the reins of his horse, and Hartack stepped into the saddle. He uttered a frightened squawk as two men stepped out of the brush not fifty feet away.

"You're wrong, Hartack," Quade said. "You're all through cutting."

Priam looked at the fence, and his voice shook as he cried, "Look what they've done!"

All that cut wire lay in a disjoined line along the ground, in lengths of about ten feet.

"Priam," Quade said sharply. He had never seen such a will to kill on a man's face.

Hartack was hanging on the brink of a decision, and Quade said, "I want you to try."

Hartack looked at those merciless eyes, and the decision was made for him. The rigidity went out of his fingers, and he carefully moved his hand away from his gunbutt.

Quade said, "Keep them covered, Priam." He stepped to a length of cut wire and picked it up by the end. It was a thorough job of cutting, wire for the length of forty posts was ruined.

He stood six feet from Hartack, holding the end of the wire in his hand. "You like barbed wire, Hartack?" he asked. He lashed his arm, and the wire whistled toward Hartack like a toothed whip. A good three feet of it wrapped around Hartack's left shoulder and neck, and those barbs bit deep. Hartack screamed, and his hands rose to the wire, trying to claw it clear. Quade jerked on the wire, and Hartack was pulled from the saddle. He jerked again, and the wire came free from Hartack's body, the barbs ripping through clothing and flesh. Hartack rolled on the ground in agony, and Quade lashed him again. He handled the length of wire like a bullwhip, and an end of it laid open Hartack's cheek. Hartack's screaming was terrible to hear. Quade lashed him again and again, tearing the shirt from his body and cross-hatching his chest and arms with deep tears. All the long, hot hours of work were in the beating.

"Quade," Priam called in a husky voice. "That's enough."

The words reached through the haze of fury in Quade's mind, and he stopped, panting hard. The wire was still wrapped about his fist, and his hand was bleeding. Hartack's screaming faded to racking sobs, and he rolled on the ground, twitching each time his lacerated flesh touched the earth.

Quade looked at Priam and saw a white line around his lips. He said, "I want him to remember this." He turned his head toward Simomns and Wesley and said, "Either of you want to cut more wire?"

They were white-faced at the brutality they had witnessed. Simmons licked dry lips and shook his head, and it was answer for both of them.

Quade tossed the wire from him. "Get him out of here. And tell MacLendon I'll kill the next man he sends against us."

Simmons climbed down and helped Hartack to his feet. Hartack moaned as the man's hands touched him. He made three attempts before he could get into his saddle, and he slumped there, bent almost double. He floated on foggy waves of pain, only half conscious.

Simmons looked at Quade before he turned his horse and shook his head. He didn't realize the awe in the gesture. Wesley looked as though he were going to be sick, and he visibly shook.

"Get," Quade snapped. He watched them ride away, Simmons leading Hartack's horse.

"Will they come back?" Priam asked huskily.

"Maybe," Quade answered. Who knew how a man would react after reflection of an incident. At the moment, those three were running, two of them scared, and one in pain. He was not close enough to hear Wesley say to Simmons, "Who's going to tell the colonel about this?"

"Not me," Simmons answered. "Hell," he said explosively. "There's other jobs." He turned his head and looked at Hartack. "I'm betting he'll say the same, when he's clear-headed enough to think about it. MacLendon wants a fight with Quade—not me."

Quade saw them change course, turning almost at a right angle to their original one. He said, "And maybe they won't." If he were right, it left the fight up to the MacLendons. Where it went from there, he did not know. The MacLendons might be convinced enough to drop it—or it could worsen. He thought of Jonse's hotheadedness, of the implacable purpose in MacLendon's eyes. He didn't think they would drop it.

He said, "Priam, I'm going to take that set of harness in to be mended. And I want to talk to Osley. The man who tells his story first always seems to have the stronger one."

Priam looked at the ruined section of fence and swore bitterly. "He won't do anything about it."

"Probably not," Quade agreed. "But he'll hear about it, anyway."

NINE

OSLEY turned a pencil in his fingers. He did not look at Quade as he was asked, "You making a formal complaint against the colonel?"

"Would it do me any good?" The sneer in Quade's voice was evident.

Osley's face turned red, and he let the question go unanswered. "Quade," he blurted out. "You can't keep on bucking the MacLendons."

"I've done all right so far." Quade shook his head in disgust. "Don't you get a little sick of the face you see when you shave? It cost Priam to build that fence. Who pays him for it? Who protects him? It's sure as hell not you." He leaned forward and stabbed a finger at Osley's face. "I don't give a damn what you believe, or how much you back the MacLendons. But nobody's going to bother the Chesbroughs any more."

The pencil kept turning in Osley's fingers. He looked like a sick man. "Somebody's going to be hurt out of this."

Quade thought of Ellis and Hartack. "Somebody already has been. But it's been the wrong ones. Maybe I can change that, too."

He strode to the door without looking around. He could expect nothing from Osley; he could expect nothing from any of them. He cursed them all.

He climbed into the wagon and drove to the harness shop at the end of the second block. He shouldered the set of harness and walked inside. A dozen rivets were missing from it, and three of the straps were broken. Others were frayed and worn and should be replaced. It would be better to throw this set away and buy a new one. But a new set cost money—money he didn't have, and money that Priam needed for other things. His face was bleak as he thought of the pinch that was in store for them in the future.

81

An old man looked up from his bench at Quade's entrance. His hair was sparse and white, and his face sagged in loose folds. His blue eyes were faded but still alert.

Bits of leather and lacing littered the floor, and the air was fragrant with the smell of new leather.

The old man said testily, "What do you want?"

The question was unnecessary, for the old man could see the worn harness on Quade's shoulder. Quade thought, he knows who I am. He'll refuse the work. There was something about the old man's voice that was familiar, but at the moment he could not place it.

He said bluntly, "I'm Jim Quade."

"You bragging about it?" the old man snapped.

Quade's eyes turned cold. "This harness needs mending. Can you fix it?"

"Can you pay for it?"

Quade breathed hard. Oh, damn this town. This was the attitude Priam had fought for so long. The old man used his age as a shield that kept Quade from reaching out and shaking some manners into him. He placed the voice now. It sounded quite a lot like Jonse MacLendon's. It had the same high-pitched tone, the same suggestion that it might break on the next word.

He growled. "You people love the MacLendons so much you even try to imitate the way they talk."

A hot spark glowed in the old man's eyes. He said shrilly, "Don't you be pointing out my voice. I was talking this way a hell of a long time before Jonse MacLendon even started."

So it had been pointed out before, and the old man resented it. Quade was taken aback at this complete reversal of what he expected. He said, "But I thought—"

"I know what you thought," the old man snapped. "I saw the chip on your shoulder the minute you came in the door. Did you think I'd get up and throw my arms around you because you're sore at the world? You put a certain kind of a thought on a man, and usually that's the kind of a thought you'll get in return."

Quade thought soberly, He's right. He said, "I'm sorry, dad."

"And I ain't your dad, either," the old man said. "I'm Hank Cameron. You call me by my name or don't call me at all."

A slow smile broke out on Quade's lips. Liking was forming in him for this testy, old man.

He dumped the harness on the floor and asked, "Hank, can you fix it?" He grinned and said, "I can pay for it."

Cameron cackled. "Set you back, didn't I?" He examined the harness with a shaking head, but he did not suggest buying a new set. Quade suspected he knew or at least guessed just how poor he and Priam were.

Cameron said, "I can make it hold out a while longer." He cut his eyes at Quade. "Put some backbone in Chesbrough, didn't you?"

Quade said soberly, "It's always been there, or he couldn't have hung on as long as he did in face of the pressure he got."

Cameron snorted. "You mean the MacLeondons. Makes me sick to see everybody bow and scrape before them. Because they got a fistful of money, does that make them better than you and me? It sure as hell don't. And that Jonse, strutting down the street like a turkey cock, with just about as much brains in him and less manners. And the colonel standing back being proud of him. They're cat-mean, all three of them. You got your hands filled. And you're a damn fool for coming in here without your gun."

Quade grinned. The old man spouted words like a geyser after he got started. Quade wanted to keep him talking. Usually the aged had a pretty keen analysis of everyone around them, an analysis corrected by earlier mistakes of judging. Frills and pomp no longer impressed them, and there was no expediency driving them. Quade thought it made a pretty good basis to judge and weigh a man.

He said, "I promised Osley I wouldn't wear one in town."

Hank Cameron was a talker, and that started him on Osley. "I don't know about him, neither," he said. "I'm beginning to do some wondering about him. Half a dozen years ago, I could have told you he was as square as any man you'd meet. Now he's beginnig to look like all the rest of us. Hiring that trigger-happy drifter, Hobart. Scurrying around to see that the MacLendons aren't unhappy."

"Hobart a killer?" Quade asked absently.

"There's some talk that he killed a couple men before

he came here, but he ain't actually killed no one here,"
Cameron said. "He is hell-fire fast with a gun, though,
and always looking to prove it."

He moved with Quade to the front of the shop. His
voice was a little wistful as he said, "I know how rough
this town's been on Chesbrough, his girl, and you. But it
ain't really a bad town. Wherever you go, you're going
to find people pretty much the same."

"Sure," Quade said gently. He felt a little embarrassed
at the old man's embarrassment for his town. To cover it,
he examined a saddle in the window. His eyes glowed as
his fingers touched the tooling on the skirt. Hank Cameron was an artist.

"Sell you that saddle for a hundred dollars, Quade."

Quade thought of the money in his pockets and shook
his head.

The old man guessed his thoughts and said irritably,
"I'll trust you for it."

Quade grinned. "You've got a better picture of my
future than some people. Maybe some day I'll come in
and get it."

A worn double-barreled shotgun stood in the corner
of the window, and Quade picked it up. Its stock was
chipped and scarred, and the bluing of its metal had
long ago faded. He saw a little rust beginning to form
around the hammers. He broke the gun, and both barrels
were loaded. The caps of the shells were dull. They
had been in here for a long time.

Cameron said, "A drunk Mexican broke into my shop
about ten years ago. Stole a bridle. I loaded her up and
been laying for him ever since." His voice was filled with
regret. "You know that thieving son never came back."

Quade laughed and started to replace the gun. His
hand remained motionless as he heard a yelling voice
from up the street, a voice filled with alarm. It was
followed a second or two later by a shot, then another.

QUADE ran out onto the walk, still carrying the gun.
His eyes swept up the street, and he saw some people
scurrying for cover and others standing motionless, as
though frozen. Two men were mounting before the bank,
and even at this distance he saw the bandannas that
obscured most of their faces.

Hank Cameron made an unnecessary statement. "They're holding up the bank," he said shrilly.

Quade saw Osley come charging around a corner, and one of the riders threw down on him. Osley flung up his hands and spun completely around before he crumpled. The report of the shot drifted to Quade. It was too far for the shotgun to reach. If the riders drove the other way out of town, he would never get close to them. But if they came this way—

He sucked in a deep breath as they lashed their horses in his direction. He ran into the middle of the street and stopped, spreading his feet wide. The thought flashed into his mind that he did not even know if this old gun would shoot, and if it did, that it might blow up in his face? Now was a hell of a time to be having those kind of thoughts.

They shot at him as they came on. A slug geysered a fountain of dirt in front of his boots, and another plucked at his sleeve, and the greedy little fingers were hot. He waited until the horses were thirty yards away before he fired. He had two shells, and he was painfully conscious of the number.

He pulled the left-hand trigger, and a rider was blasted out of his saddle as though a giant hand jerked him from it. He swiveled the gun at the other rider, and the horses were almost upon him, the riderless horse pounding alongside the other one. He could see the muddy whites of their rolling eyes and the red of their flared, distended nostrils. He pulled the other trigger, and the butt of the gun slammed back into his shoulder. The old gun had a terrific wallop. Part of the charge took the horse, and it trumpeted its pain almost in his ear. He had a quick, confused impression of man and horse falling, and he sprang aside to keep the animal from sliding into him. The rider was flung a dozen feet, and Quade got a hasty look at the blood on his face and shirt. The man struggled to sit up, and he waved the pistol in feeble, uncoordinated motions. Quade ran to him and whacked him over the head with the gunbarrel. He heard the man's tired sigh as he slumped back into the street.

Quade was breathing hard as people ran out onto the street and toward him. His scowl kept them from press-

ing in too closely about him. The air was rank with dust
from the stirred street, the raw, hot smell of blood and
freshly spilled manure.

He looked at the growing crowd and asked, "How's
Osley?"

"He caught one in the shoulder," someone answered
him.

Quade nodded. He pointed at a figure in the dust.
"This one's dead. That one's out. He'll probably need a
doctor." The injured horse squalled again, and Quade
said irritably, "Someone shoot that horse." He felt more
regret for it than he did for the riders.

He handed the shotgun to Cameron and said, "You
need more shells."

Cameron took the gun from him, and there was al-
most reverence in the way he touched it. He said,
"Quade, that was the damnedest thing I ever say.
Why—"

Quade shook his head; he did not know why himself.

He walked to the doctor's office, and Osley was on a
table. The doctor was probing for the slug, and sweat
stood out in huge drops on Osley's face. Quade watched
with detached interest. Osley's face twisted, but he did
not make a sound.

The doctor pulled out the flattened slug with a pair of
forceps and held it up for Quade to see. He said, "I
took one out of Ellis. You keep my business going good."

Osley's eyes were tight closed, and Quade thought
maybe he had fainted. He grunted with irritation. "I
had nothing to do with them hitting him."

"Sanders," Osley murmured huskily. "Can I have a
drink?"

"Sure, sure," Doc Sanders said. "I forgot." He pulled
a bottle of bourbon from a desk drawer and took a long
pull at himself before he turned to Osley. His eyes were
bright with whisky shine as he looked at Quade. "Now,
you can add me to the things you disapprove of about
this town."

Quade regarded him with steady eyes. The once-thin
face was swollen with liquor bloat. This man had wanted
to be a doctor, and he had studied long years for it.
But somewhere along the line doctoring had become
secondary, and whisky had taken over. Doc Sanders

had his own problem, and he was not living with it very well.

Quade said, "I could never disapprove of you as much as you do."

Sanders stared at him, and a flush spread over his face. He started to say something, and Osley said plaintively, "Doc, the drink."

Sanders put the bottle in Osley's hand, and the sheriff shuddered as the raw liquid bit at his throat. His eyes were watery, when he opened them. He said gruffly, "They tell me you got both of them. I'm grateful, Quade."

Quade said, "Don't let it fret you."

Four men came in through the door, carrying the wounded robber. The man was still unconscious. Quade looked at Sanders and said, "That'll keep you busy picking the shot out of him."

Sanders held out his hand, and there was only a little tremble in it. "You don't think I can do it?"

"I wouldn't know," Quade said dryly and went out the door.

He was halfway down the block, when a tall, austere-looking man stopped him. The man said, "I'm Steve Coniston." He smiled faintly. "The banker."

Quade looked at him blank-eyed.

Coniston said, "They would have made away with a sizable sum of money if you had not stopped them."

Quade held his tongue. He felt no inclination to make it easier for this man.

Coniston said, "Chesbrough was in some months ago to ask about a loan. I couldn't see my way clear then. If you would tell him to see me now—"

Quade knew a little melting. This town was not entirely ungrateful. This loan Coniston was offering could be their salvation.

Coniston looked nervously about him. He said, "I'd appreciate it if you'd tell him this is strictly between him and me."

Quade's anger flared anew. He said savagely, "You afraid the MacLendons will find out? That would be bad for you, wouldn't it? Keep your damned money." They were not in the position yet of having to accept back-handed gratitude from anyone.

He left Coniston staring after him. He admitted he had rebuffed an overture of friendliness. Maybe he was too suspicious; maybe he didn't look at the other man's side of it. If so, the town had conditioned him that way. And it was going to take a lot of conditioning for him to feel any other way.

TEN

QUADE drove the nail into the board, and his hammer strokes were vicious. He felt quarrelsome, and there was no particular reason for it. Yes, there was, he decided. He was feeling the pinch of poverty, and it left him mean and ground down. He had used every piece of scrap material on the place, and there was still a long way to go before it began to look respectable. He thought, there's a limit to how far a man can stretch things. They needed some money around this place and needed it bad. He thought wryly, I should have thrown in with those bank robbers, instead of stopping them. He wondered if anyone around here would give him a job and discarded the thought for two reasons. First, he would beg of no man, not even work, and second, he would hate to leave here, even for a limited time. He glanced at the house, and an unconscious smile was on his lips. It was odd how a man could wander lonely for so many years without any kind of pull at all, then find it strong and chain-binding without him even realizing it was going to happen at that spot. He shook his head in rebuke at himself. A broke man thinking those kind of thoughts. Suddenly he was filled with a new kind of longing—a longing for all those wasted years back, to have them over again so that he could fill them with usefulness and productivity.

He said harshly, "Quade, you'll be blubbering in a minute."

He turned his head at the rumble of wagon wheels, and relief spread over his face that Priam was back. Priam had insisted upon going into town, and Quade had let him go with a great deal of reluctance. Not that he actually feared harm would come to him—things had changed since that first night—but still, it could be pushing things a little too fast.

Priam drove into the yard, and his face was radiant. He climbed down and said, "Quade, this was the first time in months I dared drive into town in broad daylight. I tied up in front of Hamilton's store and walked in like I had a right." He shook his head at the wonder of it and said strongly, "By God! I do have the right."

Quade gathered some of the packages in the bed of the wagon. "Nothing happened?"

"Nothing. Wilkie was in town. He put those mean eyes on me, but he didn't cross the street." He said thoughtfully, "Maybe I was just a mite afraid of him but not like I used to be."

Quade grunted. Priam had come a long way since the night he first saw him in town.

"People talked to me," Priam said proudly. "Everyplace I went, they wanted to talk to me. Mostly about you and the holdup. Quade, some of the people are thinking you might be all right."

Quade briefly grinned. "But they're not sure of it, yet." Priam had bought a lot of stuff, some of it luxury items. That jar of peach preserves that spilled out of the sack—sure it would go mighty well with Susan's biscuits, but things like that could wait until they were more secure.

He said gruffly, "You spend everything you had?"

Priam grinned and dug in his pockets. He started pulling money out by the handfuls.

"Holy Mother," Quade said in awed tones. "You robbed the bank."

Priam laughed. "If I did, it was legal. I saw Coniston. He let me have a loan."

Quade's face hardened. "Did he put strings on it?" At Priam's puzzled look he said, "Did you have to sneak in a side door for it?"

Priam's face sobered. He said quietly, "We needed the money bad, Quade. It meant more than the money to me. It meant that Coniston and the others think I'm going to stay here now. Maybe I don't have as much pride as you do. But if Coniston doesn't want it known, it's all right with me."

He picked up a sack of groceries and stalked toward the house.

Quade glared after him, then his face softened. This had been Priam's big moment, and he had kicked it to pieces. He hurried after him and put hand on his shoulder. He said, "It takes more brains than I've got to know when to bend a little."

Priam's injured expression lessened. "I was only thinking of Susan, of all of us. It's going to be a considerable while before we have anything else to sell. That's too long, when you're down to counting pennies."

Quade thought a harsh oath for himself. He had been close to taking something away from Priam; he had been picking at this hard-won, new confidence. He said gruffly, "Forget it. I was wrong."

Susan came out on the porch and said, "What are you two arguing about?"

"No argument," Priam said too quickly. "I was just telling Quade the news in town."

She was not fooled, Quade thought. But she was wise enough to let the matter drop. Looking at her, Quade thought he found the source of his irritation at Priam. He wanted to be the one who brought her security.

He saw the frown grow on her face as she started putting away the groceries. She said without turning her head. "You bought pretty reckless, didn't you?"

Priam sneaked up behind her and thrust a handful of money before her eyes. She cried out and whirled, and her eyes were wide.

Priam's face was shining again. He waved the money and said, "Honey, the bank thinks we're solid enough citizens to loan us money."

She squealed with delight and threw her arms about his neck. Quade saw the glisten of tears in her eyes. He wanted to swear; he wanted to hit something. It was an ordinary sum of money, but it meant so much to her. Not the money, he thought with a sudden flash. It was the hard-won foothold the money represented.

Priam turned and looked at Quade. He said, "Susan, you know why I got the money. It's because Jim is out here with us." It was one of the rare times Priam used Quade's first name.

She said softly, "I know."

Quade felt his face getting red. He said, "I got work to do." He felt good inside. The quarrelsome edge of his temper was all gone.

"Sit down," she said. "I'll make some coffee." The

bribe was not in her words—it was in the sparkle of her eyes. She set the pot on the stove and asked, "What else is new in town?"

Don't tell her about Wilkie, Quade thought. Don't dampen this moment for her.

"A couple of kids in town are sick. Mrs. Wilson's Nancy is one of them. Both of them seem to have the same thing. Head and backaches and complaining their belly hurts."

Quade saw Susan's face go still. He thought the name Mrs. Wilson did that to her. Her voice was flat as she asked, "What does Doctor Sanders say it is?"

Priam said irritably, "He hasn't been around for a couple of days. Probably drunk somewhere."

Susan asked in a breathless voice, "Are the children getting red spots on their stomachs?"

Priam shook his head. "I didn't hear."

Quade asked quickly, "What is it, Susan?"

Her voice was frightened, and she struggled to keep the note of fear from breaking it. She said, "It sounds like typhoid. I went through an epidemic of it in St. Louis. I helped a doctor, and I learned what he looked for." She walked to a wall peg and took down her bonnet. "Father, you will have to drive me in."

Quade stared incredulously at her, and he thought, people had complimented him on his courage, when he stopped the bank holdup. That took no real courage, for action picked up a man and carried him along, leaving him no time to think. What she proposed doing took the courage. For the time to think was there, time to examine the unknown and see the terror lurking in it.

He said explosively, "Susan. No."

She gave him a faint smile. "Somebody has to do it."

There was no arguing against that simple statement. He shook his head and said, "I'll drive you in."

Priam said, "I'm going, too."

"You can't," she said. "If Jim goes, someone has to stay with Jimmy. I can't take him there."

Quade cut Priam's argument short. "She's right, Priam. I'll give her what help I can."

HE STOLE a look at her face as he drove toward town. If she knew fear or worry, she did not show it. Her face was absorbed but not frightened. He knew fear. It was drying his mouth and tightened his muscles. A man was so damned helpless up against something like this. It could be in a room, moving at a man with deadly stealth, and he could not see it nor even get his hands upon it.

He ran his tongue around his mouth and asked, "Are you sure it's typhoid?"

"Not until I see one of them. It comes from infected water, Jim. And it hits the young the hardest."

Her words did nothing to lessen his creeping fear. The 'young' could so very well include her.

He said, "I could try to find Sanders."

She laid her fingers on his arm. "I'm still going, Jim. Even if the doctor is there, he'll need all the help he can get."

He did not speak again until he reached town. He was filled with marvel at the strength in her. A man had physical strength, and by comparison, it was nothing at all. He asked, "Where do you want to go first?"

Her voice was quite steady. "Stop at Mrs. Wilson."

He shook his head but made no other protest.

Mrs. Wilson met them at the door, and her animosity was swept away in this new fear. She grasped they were there to help her, for she said in a trembling voice, "She's worse this morning."

"May I see her?" Susan asked.

Tears spilled from Mrs. Wilson's eyes and she said, "Come in." Her fat face was twisted with distress, and Quade wondered how anyone could hate this object of pity.

Mrs. Wilson led the way to the bedroom. A girl of ten or eleven tossed restlessly upon the bed. She was muttering, but her words were disconnected and senseless.

Susan bent over her, and Quade wanted to jerk her from the bedside. The air in the room was heavy and foul, the smell of sickness. The fear was twisting inside him, and he had to make a conscious effort to keep himself under control. He heard her say, "Her lips are crusted with fever," and knew Susan was talking to herself. He saw her examine the child's tongue, and it was coated with a dirty brown. She pulled up the girl's nightgown, and the stomach was swollen. When she touched it, the child cried out.

"How long has she been like this?" she asked Mrs. Wilson.

"Almost a week. I thought it was just some kind of summer complaint." Mrs. Wilson's face contorted, and she wailed, "She's going to die. Nancy's going to die."

Susan frowned at her, and Quade said sharply, "Shut up." It shocked a degree of calmness into her.

Susan said firmly, "She is not going to die," and Quade felt a new will interjected into this, a strong, determined will.

Susan said, "Bring me a basin of cold water."

She crooned to the child, while the woman was obeying her order, and it seemed to Quade Nancy's delirious muttering lessened.

When Mrs. Wilson returned, Susan said, "Watch how I do this. You will have to do it often during the next few days."

She sponged the child for better than an hour, stopping from time to time to feel Nancy's forehead. She said fretfully, "I think her temperature's less. I wish I had a thermometer."

She kept up the sponging for another hour, and it seemed to Quade the child was definitely better. Susan stood and moved her weary shoulders. "Keep it up," she said. "I'll be back later in the day." She added as an afterthought, "Don't give her any water unless it's boiled."

Mrs. Wilson grabbed her arm. "Don't go," she pleaded. "You can't leave me now."

Susan pried away her fingers. She said gently, "There are others sick."

Mrs. Wilson's hand fell away, and she drew strength from this younger woman. She asked, "You'll be back?"

"I'll be back," Susan assured her.

Quade followed her out the door. The pride he felt in this small, slim woman put an aching lump in his throat.

They found six other cases in the town, and while the parents were concerned, they were not alarmed—not until Susan told them what she suspected.

The day hours melted into the night, and there was a long weary passage of them. Quade did not know how she kept going, and she made only one complaint. "If only I knew more about this," she said.

He cursed in his helplessness, and his cursing included himself and Sanders and every worthless male.

He got a couple of hours sleep, sitting in a chair, and in the morning, the sun, touching his face, awakened him. He grunted and tried to stretch the stiffness from his muscles.

He saw Susan across the street, passing the porch on which he sat. He was quite positive she had no two hours sleep in a row. He called to her, and she turned a preoccupied face toward him. For an instant, he thought she did not even recognize him.

He ran across the street and seized her arm. Her eyes were enormous smudges in a drawn face. He said angrily, "You've got to get some rest."

If she heard him, she ignored his order. She said, "Jim, the town's well has to be sealed off."

He stared at her, and she misunderstood his expression. "Don't you understand?" she said fiercely. "The children have been drinking water from that well. It's contaminated."

The well was on the north side of town, and he had drank from it once. He thought it pretty good water then.

He said dryly, "And you want me to seal it off?"

"Why, yes," she said with a surprised look for the question. "Right away, Jim. I've got to see Nancy now."

He shook his head as he watched her move away. She was handing him a full sized riot, but she expected him to seal that well. He said a helpless, "Hell," as he moved off to find some timbers.

The well curbing was of wood, and that was going to be a help. He laid two inch thick boards across the well opening and spiked them down with the biggest nails he could buy.

Before he was half-way through, a half-dozen men gathered, and more were headed in his direction, drawn by the pounding.

He laid another board in place and set the first nail with a lick from his hammer.

One of the men asked, "What do you think you're doing?"

Quade looked at him, the hammer up-raised in his hand. "Sealing off the well," he said. He stared gravely at the man, and he shifted under his regard.

Quade saw glances exchanged among them. There was outrage in them, but that was Jim Quade doing the sealing, and they felt their way along.

"Why?" the man blurted.

"Orders," Quade said laconically.

It was an important sounding word, and no one spoke while Quade finished nailing the board. He reached for another, and the man said uncertainly, "Damnit. That's our drinking water."

"Not for awhile, it isn't," Quade said and spiked the board down.

He heard them talking among themselves, and there was heat in their words. He might finish this before they stirred themselves up enough to act.

"Where will we get our drinking water?" the man asked belligerently.

"Haul it, I guess," Quade said between hammer strokes.

The man advanced a step. Jim Quade did not mean as much as he had a few moments ago. "Damnit," the man shouted. "That's a haul of five miles."

Quade shook his head in sympathy and nailed down the last board. It was a thorough job. It would take at least a bar to pry them off. Seeing that they were not pried off would be the tough part.

H E STRAIGHTENED and faced a crowd of thirty or forty people—angry people, their faces mottled red. The half-dozen women in the crowd were as angry as the men. He thought, any second now, and I've got my riot.

A women said shrilly, "Who ordered you to seal off the well?"

Quade did not see Susan approaching, but she was close enough to hear the woman's question.

"I did," she said calmly.

Quade silently cursed. She could not have picked a worse time to appear.

"You've got a lot of nerve," someone in the crowd shouted. Angry voices rose backing his statement.

"Hold it," Quade said sharply. They were out-raged and angry, and their tongues could run away under it. He did not want anyone shouting a barb at her. If they did, he would have to wade in and whip the whole crowd.

She said earnestly, "You've got a typhoid epidemic on your hands. The disease came from this well. Do you want more of your children sick? They will be, if you let them drink this water?"

That struck a note of fear in them, and they fell to muttering among themselves. Then someone, in the rear of the crowd, said in a jeering voice, "How do you know? You're no doctor."

That was the weak spot, Quade thought. And if they pushed against it, it would give. People were the damnest things, he thought savagely. The posing and posturing of a hopeless charlatan would impress them, but they would question someone else's word—as long as there was not a reputation behind that word.

A woman yelled, "Are you going to let them shut off our well?" and the crowd surged forward.

"Stay back," Quade called sharply. If he had to, he would break a few heads with the hammer.

He saw Osley come around the corner and knew no relief. Osley's presence could make the matter worse. For if Osley sided with the crowd, there was no possible chance of stopping them.

Osley pushed through the crowd and demanded, "What's all this about?"

A dozen voices answered him, and Osley roared, "Damnit. One at a time."

Susan's expression was very intent. "Sheriff," she said. "This water's contaminated. You'll have to find another source. And even that should be boiled. You know how many children are sick here. Do you want more?"

Osley said uneasily, "Are you sure?"

"Yes," she said, and the positive factor in her voice could not be denied.

Osley turned and faced the crowd. "This well stays sealed," he declared. "She's here trying to help you. Did any of the rest of you do anything before she came? I'll jail the first one I see tampering with these boards. Go on about your business."

This was authority, and the crowd's determination weakened under it. The people, in the rear, turned and moved away, and it left the ones in the front rank naked under Osley's glare.

They, too, turned, and the last man away muttered, "It's going to be a hell of a chore, hauling water."

Quade sighed. He owed Osley a revision in his thinking about him.

Osley looked at him and grumbled, "You could have come to me first."

Quade grinned. "It didn't occur to me," he said honestly. "Will your warning keep them away?"

A bleak humor was in Osley's eyes. "Stobie ain't very busy now. I'll put him to watching it." His voice grew gruff. "They're mad. But they'll be grateful, once they do a little thinking."

Quade waited until Osley was moving away before he spoke to Susan. "That was close," he said.

She gave him a wan smile. "Yes," she agreed.

She started away, and Quade said, "Can't you rest a little, now?"

"Later," she called over her shoulder.

His face was concerned as he watched her go. She was killing herself for a damned, ungrateful town, and he was helpless to change any phase of it. He looked at the well and cursed it, then a small grin broke out on his lips. He was thinking of Stobie Hobart sitting out in the hot sun watching a boarded-up well.

During the next five days, Quade did not know when Susan slept. What food she ate had to be almost forced upon her. He raged at the toll it demanded of her; he watched her grow more hollow-cheeked and big-eyed with each passing hour. But those were only outward manifestations—the inner strength of will never weakened.

He drove out to the house and got clean clothing for her, and she absently thanked him. There was room for nothing else in her mind but those sick children. She became a familiar sight to the town, going tirelessly from one house to the other, and Quade thought soberly, more than the little knowledge she has about it, it's her determination that's holding them together. Five new cases were added during that time, and three of the children died. Through repetition, Quade learned to recognize the dreaded signs of approaching death. The child's exhaustion deepened, and there was vomiting of blood. The stomach pains would increase until the patient screamed with them. The pulse would flicker, and the skin would grow cold and clammy. A rapid fall in temperature marked the onrushing end. Then he saw the defeat in her face and the quick rush of tears to her eyes. The funerals were bad, for a man's head was filled with unanswered questions. He stood at the graveside and thought of the unfulfilled years that belonged to each of the small victims, and he could not blame the parents for their bitterness in their loss.

Her defeat never lasted long, for there was always another patient to turn to, and the despair was swept away in a new urgency. She worked hardest with Nancy, and perhaps unconsciously her love was greater, for the child was her first patient. There was dumb reverence on Mrs. Wilson's face, whenever she looked at Susan, and Quade knew that never again would the woman cause Susan anguish.

He found a grudging liking for this town building in him and knew it was built of a shared emergency. He stood in front of the Orient Saloon, talking to Osley and a half-dozen of the townsmen. He was tired—he felt it in the deep, bone-aching weariness of both his legs.

One of the men said in awe, "There she goes again. How in the hell does she keep up?"

It voiced the question in Quade's mind as he watched Susan disappear into a house. He shook his head and let it be answer enough.

The man chuckled and said, "She's the boss-man in this town. When she puts those eyes on you and tells you to do something, you jump. Look at the way she had the big well sealed off. I never thought she could do that." A hope was in his voice as he said, "You know, I think it might be starting to end. There hasn't been a new case in the last couple of days."

Osley said, "This town was damned lucky to have her around."

He flushed under Quade's cynical look, and he repeated it stubbornly enough. "Well it is."

Gillian spat a gob of tobacco juice into the dust and said, "The MacLendons sure stayed clear, once they heard we had typhoid here. I guess the Colonel was afraid to risk having his sons around."

There was a murmur of harsh assent around the circle, and Quade thought, this has done some good. It had demanded a terrible price from her, but she had accomplished what cursing and fists and bullets could never do.

One of the men looked up and said, "Well I'll damned. Here comes Doc Sanders."

He started forward, and Osley seized his arm.

The man said in objection, "I'm going to ask that bastard where he's been, while he was needed."

"Later," Osley said. "Don't stop him now. He's got work to do."

None of them waved or said a word as Sanders rode past. He sat slumped in the saddle, and his clothing was stained and rumpled. His eyes were dull, and his face looked more bloated than usual. He's been on a long drunk, Quade thought.

The group stayed where it was, watching Sanders visit the houses of the patients. After the first one, Susan was with him. Quade would have given a lot to hear their conversation. At the end of an hour, Sanders approached them. His face colored at the lack of greeting, and he said abruptly, "The girl has done a remarkable job. She did about everything I could do. We know too little about it. Some day—" He shook his head and said, "There's still danger for some of the children, but I think they'll pull through."

Quade said harshly, "She's dead-beat. Can you take over?"

A mocking smile pulled at Sanders' lips. "I can take over."

Osley asked bluntly, "Where you been?"

Sanders answered in an equally blunt voice, "Drunk. Dead drunk. At the MacLendons."

His head lifted, and his eyes narrowed at the expressed anger in the group. "I just learned this morning what was happening here. I wondered why the Colonel insisted I stay so long. But his whisky was good." He made a vague gesture. "I was content to let it go at that. I know now he wanted me near, in case anyone got sick at his house. But I was flattered at the big man's wanting me." A smile formed on his lips, bitter and self-mocking. "You see, I'm suffering from the same disease everyone in this town has."

"What's that?" Osley asked harshly.

"Bankruptcy of principle," Sanders answered and walked away.

None of the men spoke. They stood in uneasy silence, then drifted away. Quade felt a little sorry for them. When a man got a clear look at himself and found the view bad, there was no place to run and hide.

ELEVEN

WILKIE watched his brother with sullen eyes, Jonse was half drunk before they started to town, and the old man did not jump all over him. Wilkie thought with a sudden burst of rage, Jonse can do anything.

The horses danced impatiently, while Jonse tilted up the bottle. The bottle neck clattered against his teeth, and he swore and jerked on the reins. "Stand still, damn you," he yelled.

Wilkie looked at the tilted-up bottle, and saliva started in his mouth. "Save me a drink," he yelled.

His words came just as Jonse flung the drained bottle from him. Jonse turned his bright, mocking smile upon him. "Wilkie," he drawled. "You never do speak up in time for anything. But don't you worry. Ole Jonse is going to buy you a drink when we get to town."

Rage made Wilkie's lips tremble. This 'ole Jonse' routine was fairly new, but Jonse used it with a frequency that made Wilkie went to scream at him. It sounded as though Jonse was the older brother, and he was looking after a half-witted younger one. It amused the Colonel, and Wilkie thought, damn him, too. Someday, I'll show both of them.

He lifted the reins, half tempted to turn back. He did not think it too wise, riding into town right now, for the MacLendons did not stand as high as they formerly had. A little caution never hurt anyone, but Jonse did not know the meaning of the word.

He must have guessed Wilkie's thoughts, for his eyes sparkled with a wicked glint. "You afraid to ride into town, Wilkie? Well, don't you be. Ole Jonse will take care of you."

"Shut up," Wilkie said savagely.

Jonse chortled and rocked back and forth in the saddle.

He was pretty drunk, Wilkie observed. That last slug had hit him hard. He hope it would hit him harder. He hoped Jonse would fall out of the saddle. By God, if he did, Wilkie would let him lay right in the middle of the road.

Jonse's face turned mean with the lightning change of a drunk's mood. "I'll show them, if they think they're too good for us," he muttered. "When I was in yesterday, some of them looked at me with spit in their eyes. They spoke to me, but it was because they were afraid not to." He looked at Wilkie and shouted, "Do you hear me? They're afraid not to speak to me."

Wilkie stirred uneasily. He wanted to get Jonse off this line of thinking, or it could stir up big trouble. He asked, "Jonse, how come nobody's ridden by to hire on with us? We gotta get some help pretty soon." He thought morosely, By God, they had to have it. He was not going to keep on working the way he had been. A month ago, a dozen men would have been clamoring for a job with the MacLendons. Now, they could not hire even a kid.

Jonse turned burning eyes on him. "It's that damned Quade," he said. "Everybody's afraid of him. "You, most of all."

"That's a damned lie," Wilkie shouted.

Jonse's eyes gleamed bright. This was an old needle, but it had a long point. "You are," he said solemnly. "I've seen you cross the street to avoid meeting him. When he knocked you down, what did you do? You lay there and bawled like a baby."

"It's a lie." Wilkie raised his voice to its fullest volume as though by shouting he could drown out Jonse's words. "He had a gun on me."

"He didn't have a gun on you," Jonse taunted. "You were just afraid to get up."

Wilkie's face was wild. He had been spurred too often by Jonse. If Jonse did not stop it, he was going to kill him some day.

He said, "You're as afraid of him as anybody else."

The remark scraped Jonse' hide thin. "The hell I am," he shouted. "I just hope he's in town. I'll show you. I'll show every son-of-a-bitch there."

He quirted his horse into a dead run, and Wilkie let

him pull ahead. Hope flooded him. Jonse was drunk and mad enough that he might face Quade. Wilkie said aloud, "I hope he does. By God! I just hope he does."

As Quade helped Susan from the wagon she said, "You're a born cynic, Jim. Look how they waved and called to us as we drove in."

The sparkle was back in her eyes. It was remarkable how fast she recuperated. Seeing her now, Quade could not believe she had looked so worn and haggard just a few days ago. He said moodily, "A town's just people. Right now, our side of the wheel has come around, and they like us. But that wheel keeps on turning."

She laughed and said, "You can't spoil my day. It's good to be liked. Mrs. Wilson asked me to stop in for tea the next time I was here." Her chin lifted. "I'm going to. I want to see Nancy."

"Sure," he said. He wanted to tell her not to put away all her defenses, that because one did not see a cat's claws did not mean they were not there. Maybe she was right—maybe he was a born cynic.

She asked, "Why don't you come with me?"

"Me?" he said with shock. "For tea?" He saw the twinkle in her eyes and knew she was teasing him. He grinned and said, "Lord, wouldn't I fit well at a tea party."

"I like you so much better, when you smile," she said.

Their eyes locked and held, and all the unspoken words flashed back and forth between them. Her voice was unsteady as she said, "Why don't you go have a beer, Jim? I won't be too long."

"Don't," he said gruffly. "Or it'll be after dark when we get home."

He turned and walked away. The word 'home' rang in his head. It had a nice sound, a soul-satisfying sound. He looked back, and she still stood there. He raised his hand in a wave, and she answered it. Then she abruptly turned and went quickly down the walk.

He made his way to the Orient Saloon, and busy thoughts crammed his head. The unspoken words, inside him, were going to have to be said, and from the look in her eyes, he did not think he would find her unresponsive. Just contemplating it put a shake in his muscles.

He stepped inside the saloon, adjusting his eyes to the shadowy interior after the glare in the street. Four men were in the place, and Jonse MacLendon was one of them. Quade would have picked another place, but it was too late. All those eyes were upon him, and leaving now would be an admission—an admission he did not feel.

He moved to the end of the bar and stood a dozen feet from Jonse, just as far away as he could get. He was stiff with resentment at the arrogant appraisal in Jonse's eyes, and he thought, simmer down. A man's look never hurt anyone.

He ordered his beer and was just tasting it, when Jonse said in a loud voice, "Beer. Now isn't that a hell of a drink for a man."

Again Quade was struck with the adolescent note in Jonse's voice. He thinks like one, too, he thought furiously.

A couple of snickers followed Jonse's remark. Quade felt the back of his neck getting hot. He kept his eyes straight ahead.

Jonse said, "Quade, throw that damned stuff away. I'll buy you a real drink."

Quade put a brief look upon him. Jonse was very drunk. It was in the bright shine of his eyes, in the flush of his face. Even motionless, there was a suggestion of a weave in him.

Quade said, "Thanks, no. I'll stick to my beer."

He watched Jonse in the back mirror. He hoped the young fool had enough remaining sense to let this stop where it was.

Jonse's face turned ugly. "I'm going to buy you that drink," he said stubbornly.

Quade turned and faced him. "I'll drink what I want and with whom I please." That was as blunt as he could make it, and he did not have too much concern whether or not it rasped Jonse.

The pupils of Jonse's eyes contracted to pin-points. He breathed gustily, then he said, "You think you're too good to drink with a MacLendon."

"I didn't say that."

Jonse sensed an advantage, and he pushed it. "You meant it," he said shrilly.

Quade saw that Jonse intended upon taking this all

the way. He probably had from the moment Quade entered. He placed both hands on the bar, keeping his elbows away from his body. The young fool could see he was not armed.

It went against the grain, but he said, "We'll make it some other time, Jonse."

To Jonse it was an admission of weakness, and he said, "No, God-damn it. We'll make it right now." He rocked back and forth, and his face had a triumphant shine. "You know what I think, Quade. I think you're a yellow dog. I think you built up your reputation by back-shooting. When a man faces you, you start crawling."

There was a white line around Quade's lips. Rage was a seething cauldron within him. He kept his mouth shut.

"Jonse," one of the men said uneasily. "He's not wearing a gun. Easy, Jonse."

"I've got two," Jonse said. "He can have one of mine." He jerked the left-hand gun from its holster and laid it on the bar. His laugh cut like a rasp. "There it is, Quade. Pick it up."

Quade could not trust his tongue to speak. The best thing he could do was to get out of here. He started away from the bar, and Jonse came toward him fast. The heel of Jonse's palm slammed into his shoulder, knocking him back.

"That's about enough," Quade said in a measured voice.

"Why, I haven't started yet." Jonse looked at the other men and grinned. He was backing down the great Quade. The town would be talking about this for months to come.

He drew his other gun, and Quade watched him with concern. The fool was drunk enough to pull the trigger.

Jonse said, "You'll pick up that gun, or crawl out the door on your hands and knees. One of the two, Quade." He thumbed the loads out of the cylinder and bounced them in his hand. Then he put one back and spun the cylinder. His eyes never left Quade's face. He put the other load in at random. "You got another choice, Quade." He spun the cylinder again. "You can stand there until the hammer finds a filled chamber."

He pulled the trigger, and the click was startingly

loud in the hushed room. He whirled the cylinder with his left thumb. He said mockingly, "Crawl, pick up that gun, or stand there. One way or another, I'm going to get you, Quade."

Quade breathed deep. Two of the six chambers were loaded. It was just a matter of time until the hammer found a loaded one. Jonse did not realize how close he was to being a dead man. For if Quade grabbed up the gun, and Jonse's trigger found another empty chamber, Jonse would not have enough time to pull the trigger again. Even with his all-consuming rage, Quade did not yet want to kill him. But he could not just stand here—and the other two choices were as unacceptable.

He said, "Jonse—"

Jonse pointed the pistol at Quade's face. "Begging isn't going to do you any good."

Quade sprang toward him as Jonse's finger tightened on the trigger. He heard the click as the hammer fell on an empty chamber. He had used all the luck coming to him. Jonse let out a startled squawk as Quade's up-swinging arm hit his gun hand. The hand was knocked up and to his right, and he tried to swing it back into line.

Quade hit him in the mouth. His pent-up rage exploded, and the blow was cruelly powerful. It knocked Jonse back into the bar, and his knees unlocked, spilling him to the floor. He still held the gun, and Quade ran to him and kicked it out of his hand.

Jonse lay against the base of the bar, dazedly shaking his head. Blood streaked across his chin and stained his shirt-front.

Quade reached down and grabbed hold of his shoulders. He hauled Jonse to his feet, and Jonse's hands clawed at his wrists. Quade slugged Jonse in the face. He let go of Jonse, and Jonse fell again. He lay on the floor, staring upward at Quade with swimming eyes, and there was a lick of comprehension in them.

"Get up," Quade snapped. He was in the grip of a murderous rage, and the only release for it was to hit Jonse as many times as he could.

Jonse tried, but his movements were feeble and uncoordinated. Quade helped him by grabbing his arm and jerking him to his feet. Jonse dove forward in a clumsy dive. Quade side-stepped, and Jones's shoulder brushed his belly. Quade brought his fist down like a mallet, hitting Jonse on the back of the head. Jonse went flat on his face and slid a little. When he lifted his head to look at Quade, his face was raw and skinned.

He had animal courage. He was hurt, but he still struggled to get to his feet. Quade chopped a right into Jonse's head just as he was straightening. The blow was a string, jerking Jonse's feet from under him. It took him longer to get up this time.

"Come on," Quade said. His anger was not nearly satisfied.

He knocked Jonse down three more times and knew a grudging admiration. Jonse possessed no skill, no ability, but he did have raw courage. That courage was costing him a fearful beating. His face was bloody, and one eye was closing. He breathed gustily through parted lips, and a gap showed in his teeth. He tried to push himself up with his arms, and they folded under him. He fell forward on his face and was still.

Quade panted hard. His fists hurt, and for the first time, he noticed a cut on the knuckles on his right hand. Jonse's teeth must have done that.

He looked at the awed faces of the men and said, "When he comes to, tell him I'll kill him, if he ever crosses me again."

He guessed the rage was not all dissipated. His statement came from the last remnants of it, but he would not retract it. He crossed the floor and parted the doors. He turned his head, and Jonse had not moved. He thought MacLendon would be wild, when he heard about this. His unfinished beer still stood on the bar. He shook his head. He had come in here for a cooling beer, and now look at him. It was hell how a man's intentions got changed.

Jonse had to hold onto the horn to stay in the saddle. Even in the darkness, Wilkie could see that his face was puffy and one eye was swollen shut. Jonse ran his tongue around the inside of his cut mouth and swore. The first word released a torrent of swear words, all directed at Quade.

Wilkie chortled and said, "You sure showed him. You

showed everybody. Damn it. I would miss it. I wanted to see how you showed him."

Jonse's good eye gleamed malevolently at him. "Shut up," he said. The missing teeth gave him a lisp.

Wilkie laughed so hard that he missed the savage warning in Jonse's good eye. "He pulled your tail feathers. You won't be strutting around so much now. You won't—" His words ended in a startled squawk. For Jonse reined his horse to a stop and drew a pistol. Its muzzle was leveled on Wilkie's belly.

"I said, shut up." Jonse's lisp was not funny—not with the insane look on his face and the drawn gun in his hand. "He hit you once, and you quit. I tried to get up. I tried until I couldn't try anymore." That tiny shred of pride was all that was left Jonse, and he fiercely clutched it. "It isn't over yet. I'm not through with him. If you ever open your mouth to me again about this, I swear I'll kill you."

Wilkie said sullenly, "You can say any damn thing you want to me. But if I say one word—"

Jonse's eye was icy cold. He lifted the pistol a couple of inches and said, "Go on, Wilkie. Say that word."

His look and tone put real terror in Wilkie's heart. Jonse meant it—Jonse was damned near to killing him right now. He raised a hand in a pleading gesture and said, "Jonse, I'm not saying anything. I'm forgetting anything happened at all."

Jonse put away his gun. "Keep it that way." He moved his horse out ahead of Wilkie.

Wilkie's terror was being replaced with a murderous hate. It was not fair, Jonse being able to say anything he wanted, then putting a restriction on him. And by God, he was not going to stand for it. He meant that about killing me, Wilkie thought. I saw it in his face. The whisky, he had drunk in town, was like a hot whip in his veins, flogging his thoughts along a certain line. He hated Jonse with a savage intensity; he had always hated him. Jonse would kill him one day for sure. Wilkie had seen how easily he looked for an excuse. The hatred beat in his head like a great drum, and each stroke pounded, kill, kill, kill. He would only be saving his own life, if he did. A man had a right to do that.

He lifted the reins and moved after Jonse. When he was four feet behind him, he drew his gun and yelled, "God-damn you, Jonse. Don't you be thinking you can always tell me what to do."

Jonse was just beginning to turn his head, when Wilkie pulled the trigger. The shot hit Jonse in the middle of the back. He reared high in the saddle, looking inches taller than he usually did. The horse plunged from under him, and Jonse fell into the dust. He fell like a limp bundle of rags, and there was no movement from him after he landed. He did not even try to raise his face from the dust.

Wilkie sawed on the reins, bringing his horse under control. He had to turn it in a complete circle and force it back toward the motionless form. Wilkie was not fooled. That Jonse was a sly one—he was only waiting his chance at Wilkie. Wilkie put two more shots into Jonse's back, and his face was alight with his gloating.

"Damn you, Jonse," he yelled. "Don't you ever be talking to me the way you did."

He kept watching the body as though he half expected Jonse to rise, and a realization slowly washed into his mind. He looked back toward the town, and the two miles covered put it out of sight. He looked ahead, and the road was empty.

"I had to do it," he muttered. "He would've killed me for sure."

A new fear was stealing into his mind. The Colonel would be a crazy man, when he learned of this. He would not give Wilkie a chance to explain; he would shoot him down like a dog.

"Get up, Jonse," he shouted. "Get up."

Jonse was not going to get up. Wilkie shook so that he could hardly put the gun away. All the commands in the world could not get Jonse out of that dust. He had better run for it, before the Colonel learned what happened. He half lifted the reins, and his eyes gleamed as the thought struck him. Quade killed Jonse. He had laid for Jonse after that fight and shot him down. Wilkie had driven him off, but he had not been able to hit him. The town would believe it; the town was looking for anything to believe against Quade. And the Colonel would believe it. He might even look upon Wilkie with a little more favor.

He put a final look on the body. "Jonse," he muttered. "You done me the first good turn in your life."

He turned the horse and spurred it into a run. He wanted to race into town after a posse to go after Quade. Quade had to be run down for killing his brother. Wilkie was beginning to half believe it, himself.

TWELVE

QUADE was tugging off a boot, when he heard the pound of hoofs on the road before the house. There were several horses by the sound, and he did not like the urgency in it. They might be riding on by, and again they might not. He stamped the boot back on and reached his gunbelt down from the peg. He buckled it on and picked up Wrangle's saddle. He had the horse saddled and bridled, by the time the riders pulled to a stop before the house. He led Wrangle out the back door of the barn and ground tied him. Then he slipped along the side of the barn until he reached a front corner. In the darkness, he could not be sure, but it looked as though a dozen horsemen milled about before the house. When that many men came calling at this hour, it could mean nothing but trouble.

A light went on in the house, and its faint glow did not reach out far enough for Quade to identify any of the horsemen. His concern grew. That was a foolish thing for Priam to do. He thought of Susan and the boy in the cabin, and the sickness of worry filled his head. Was that MacLendon out there, striking back in quick retaliation for Jonse's whipping, and could he have gotten that many men to ride with him? Knowing the fickle vagaries of men's humor, Quade suspected he could have.

A voice bellowed, "Chesbrough! Come out here."

A little of the tension left Quade as he recognized the voice. That was Stobie Hobart, and at least, the semblance of legality was on this group.

Quade could not see Priam, but he could easily pick out the alarm in his voice as he asked, "What is it? What is it?"

"We want Quade," Hobart bawled. "He killed Jonse MacLendon earlier this evening."

Quade said a soundless 'ah'. He did not know what had happened, and he could not stay to find out—not with that many riders here. At the moment, the ah

112

covered everything. As he slipped back along the side of the barn he heard Hobart yell, "Turn him over, Chesbrough, or we'll tear the place apart looking for him."

Quade picked up Wrangle's reins, and keeping the barn between him and the house, led the horse away. He changed directions, when a rise in the ground hid him, quartering to the north. He did not stop until he reached higher ground, then he dropped Wrangle's reins again and lay down. The house and outbuildings were dark smudges against the black of the night, and pinpoints of light moved about them, made by either torches or lamps. He watched the search with a resigned acceptance not even particularly tinged with bitterness. Today, he had been warmly greeted in town. Tonight, a posse from the same town hunted him. People went the way the wind shoved them, and this was a powerful wind blowing tonight. He supposed this search was some kind of an aftermath of his fight with Jonse, and he speculated upon what could have happened. He discarded the thought that Jonse had died as a result of the beating. Jonse was a young, healthy animal, and his breathing had been strong, when Quade left him. No, something had happened that Quade did not know about. He wondered if Osley was with the posse. If so, the man was letting Hobart take all the lead, and that posed another unanswered question. Quade remembered his warning to Osley that Hobart wanted his job. Perhaps Hobart had decided this was the time to start.

He waited patiently for the better part of an hour, watching the dots of light move about. Those men were doing a thorough job of searching the place. Quade was afraid Chesbrough and Susan were taking abuse, but he could do nothing about it now.

He saw the points of light come together and cluster, then they went out. He grinned bleakly at the thought of the suggestions and rejections that must be flying about the group. The horsemen moved off to the southwest. They were too far away for him to hear the sound of hoofs, but he could see the darker mass moving against the black back-drop of the night. He remained where he was for a long interval. Another question probed at him with a long, irritating finger. Had all of them left, or was one or more of them stationed down there upon the possibility of his return? He decided against it. He was supposed to have killed a man, an important man, and he should be fleeing. Not finding him here, the posse would look for him elsewhere.

He led Wrangle back toward the barn, and he hesitated a long moment before he left the horse. A hunted man, on foot, felt so damned helpless.

He circled the barn and could see no one. But they might be inside. He listened for the sound of a horse or horses and heard a blubbery snort come from the barn. But that could be Priam's old horse. A light was still on in the house as he moved toward it. Another circle of it disclosed nothing, and he decided all of the posse was gone. He discarded none of his caution as he stepped to the back door on cat-feet. He tapped gently upon it and did not have to repeat it.

The door opened, and Priam peered out.

"It's Quade," he said and stepped back into the shadows. "Did they all leave?"

"I think so," Priam muttered and came out into the night.

He clutched Quade's arm and said, "They say you killed Jonse MacLendon. They say you shot him in the back."

"Who says it?"

Priam shook his head. "Why, all of them I guess."

"Did Osley make the charge?"

"He wasn't with them."

That was damned odd, unless Osley was already out of office. If so, Hobart moved fast.

A hopelessness was in his voice as Priam said, "You'll have to run for it. They'll shoot you on sight."

With his reputation, Quade supposed they would. Not a man in that posse would give him the slightest chance.

Susan came to the door and cried, "What is it, father?" A strain made her voice ragged.

"Susan," Quade called softly.

She came running toward him, and he sensed the crying in her. It seemed the most natural thing in the world that she run into his arms and that he wrap those arms about her.

He felt the wetness of her cheek pressed against his, and he said gently, "Stop it. Nothing's happened."

"They'll kill you, Jim," she sobbed.

He said with an attempt at humor to relieve her

anguish, "They've got to catch me first." That made her crying worse, and he could feel her body shaking against his. He said flatly, "I didn't kill Jonse."

"I know that," she wailed. "But they won't listen to you. Now, you'll have to leave. And I can't stand—" Her crying broke into the rest of her words.

WONDER flooded him, and he guessed he was dumb not to have been positive before now. But if there was any doubt in his mind, her words swept it away. He put a finger under her chin and tilted up her face. He said, "You don't think I could go very far, do you?"

Her cry was choked as she raised her lips to his. It was a gentle kiss, telling each what they needed to know. There was no demand nor hunger in it—that would come later, if the future were ever assured.

He raised his head and said, "I'll need some coffee and flour, Susan. Put in some salt and matches." He shook his head at several of her suggestions. He wanted to be able to move light and free, while he worked this out. He would have to stop and pick up his bed-roll out of the barn.

While she was gone, Priam asked, "Where will you start?"

Quade did not know. Right now, there seemed to be no starting point. He said, "You and Susan stay out of town." He could not be around to protect them, and the veering wind could lash against everything that was connected with Jim Quade.

She came back with a small sack, and unhappiness clouded her face. "It's so little we're doing for you," she wailed.

"You're waiting for me," he said simply. He made it sound like the greatest treasure in the world, and it was.

He kissed her again before he melted into the darkness. "I don't know when I'll be back," he said. "But I'll be around."

A great rebelliousness flooded him. A man found what he wanted, then he had to leave.

He lashed the bed-roll behind the saddle and stowed the meager supplies in the saddle-bags. A voice, behind him, said, "Quade."

He whirled, cursing his carelessness. She had filled

his mind so that it bemused his thinking. He expected to hear the boom of a gun before he was half-way around, and his flesh was tensed in anticipation of a bullet.

His gun was in his hand as he saw the figure coming toward him.

"It's Osley," the figure said.

"Don't make me shoot you," Quade said flatly.

"I hope not. Put it away, Quade. I didn't have to call out to you." A wry amusement was in Osley's voice. "I been waiting here for you to finish at the house. A man hates to interrupt that kind of work."

Quade lowered his gun, and his bewilderment showed in his tone. He said. "You're not with the posse."

"Now, that's a brilliant observation," Osley said dryly. "No, Stobie's leading it." His tone was reflective. "Stobie's shooting at two birds. He wants to get you, and he wants to get my job. You saw it right at the first."

Hope was nibbling at Quade's defense. "I didn't kill Jonse."

"I don't think so, either," Osley said calmly.

Quade stared at him. "But that posse—"

"I couldn't stop it. Wilkie rode into town and reported he saw you shoot Jonse. He ran you off, but he couldn't stop you. Jonse was shot three times in the back. Any one of them was enough. I never heard you back-shooting a man, and I never heard of you wasting ammunition."

Quade said bitterly, "They believed Wilkie." Yesterday, the MacLendons were the most unpopular people in town. Now, they were back on top of the heap.

"They believed him." Osley shook his head. "People don't remember too long, Quade. Something new comes along and they forget the old. The MacLendons had a longer hold on them than you did. Besides, it's hard for people to accept—a brother killing a brother."

"It was done before," Quade said. "A long time ago."

"Sure," Osley agreed. "And it's been done since. And it never fails to shock people."

"How come you didn't believe it?" Quade asked challengingly.

Osley seemed to ignore the question. "I figure it was Wilkie. It has to be. Probably some kind of a drunken quarrel. But the proof—" He shrugged, and it was too much answer. "Right now, you wouldn't stand a chance of even getting to a trial. And if you did, a jury would convict you. Just on Wilkie's word." He picked up Quade's question. "How come I didn't believe it? It would have been a lot easier. But there were facts to look at and something that Doc Sanders said that kept running through my mind." He grinned bleakly and said, "Maybe I'm trying to throw off the disease Doc said the town had."

Quade remembered the words, then. Bankruptcy of principle. He did not feel nearly as alone nor as helpless. He muttered, "Thanks, Osley."

"I don't know what I can do," Osley warned. "I'm bucking public opinion, but I'll try to get a rope around it. You stay out of sight." He grinned and went on, "I figure you won't go too far away. I'll try to let you know what's happening." His face sobered. "When this calms down a little and people start thinking again, maybe this will change." His tone carried a good deal of doubt. "But with Stobie stirring them up—" He did not finish the thought. "You go on up into the foothills and wait."

Quade said, "If I could get to Wilkie—"

Osley said sharply, "Don't go messing this up more than it is. Wilkie's going to stay close to people. You want to be able to come back, don't you?"

Quade nodded and turned toward Wrangle. Osley was right. But that waiting was going to be a killing job.

THIRTEEN

MACLENDON paced the floor of the parlor, his face stamped with the bitter lines of a man who has known an unbearable loss. He stopped before a rack of horns over the stone mantel and gazed at it long. He said, "Jonse shot that buck." Wilkie was in the room, but MacLendon was not talking to him. He had even forgotten Wilkie was here.

The sullen lines around Wilkie's mouth were more pronounced. This was not going as he expected, for his father would not forget Jonse. Over a week had passed since Jonse's death, and MacLendon could talk of nothing else. It was driving Wilkie crazy. He said aggrievedly, "I helped Jonse tote that buck off the mountain side." Hell! That rack of horns would not be hanging over the mantel, if it had not been for him.

His father flashed him a disgusted look, then looked at the horns again.

Wilkie poured whisky into a water glass. He filled it half full and sloshed it about before he raised it to his lips. He took a long swallow, and MacLendon turned and saw him. "Will you stop that damned drinking?" he shouted.

Wilkie put down the glass, and his face was flushed. "You never used to holler at Jonse for drinking."

MacLendon's eyes were cold. "Jonse drank like a gentleman. He could hold his liquor."

Wilkie's eyes flamed, and he looked away before the Colonel could see the naked rage in them. All he heard any more was Jonse, Jonse, Jonse. It made him sick to his stomach. He almost wished that damned Quade hadn't shot— He stopped the thought with a little wonder. If a man repeated something long enough, he got to believing it. He grinned craftily. What would the old man say, if he knew the truth? A little shiver ran along

118

Wilkie's skin. He would never want the Colonel finding out.

MacLendon said, "If I could only get my hands on Quade. I'd take a week to kill the dirty dog."

Wilkie said sullenly, "You might as well forget it. He's gone, and he's too smart to come back." His father better forget it and get back to work. He had not even gotten around to hiring a new crew, and what work was being done fell on Wilkie. He was getting damned sick and tired of it.

Wide cracks appeared in MacLendon's icy surface. "You'd like me to forget it. You'd sit around and do nothing about finding your brother's killer. If it was the other way around, Jonse would not be sitting here swilling down whisky. I almost wish—" He did not finish the sentence.

Wilkie's face turned livid. He knew what was in his father's mind. "Say it," he shouted. "You wish it was me instead of Jonse. That's what you're thinking."

His eyes wavered before MacLendon's hard stare, and he looked away. He finished the glass of whisky and poured another. He gulped it down, and the fiery force of it took the last hobble off his tongue. All his life he had to bottle up things for fear of displeasing his father or Jonse. That was gone now.

"Let me tell you something," he yelled. "I'm not sorry he's gone. All he did was devil me. And you let him. You always did favor him."

MacLendon grabbed a pistol from the mantel and whirled. He pointed it at Wilkie, and what Wilkie saw in his face filled his mind with icy fear. His face turned ashen, and he mumbled, "Paw, I didn't mean that. I didn't—"

"You meant it," MacLendon said. "You think with Jonse being dead you'll get his share of the ranch. That's all his death means to you. Maybe you will and maybe you won't. But I warn you, Wilkie. You ever say again what you just said, and you won't live long enough to get anything. I'll kill you, Wilkie. I promise you that." He kept the gun pointed at Wilkie, and his eyes backed up every word he said.

Wilkie was scared—it showed in the tremble of his hands. He looked at the floor for two reasons—to get

away from looking into his father's eyes, and to keep
MacLendon from reading the thoughts that were behind
his own.

MacLendon put the pistol back on the mantel. "Get
out of my sight," he said. "I can't stand to look at you
anymore tonight."

Wilkie rose to his feet. The whisky, he had taken, was
working hard, for he had to throw out a hand to the
table-top to steady himself. He looked at his father's
back, and a child's unreasoning grief seized him. His
own father wanted to kill him. It was true—it had been
too naked in his eyes. And he intended cutting him off
without anything. He had said as much in so many
words.

Rage was beginning to work on Wilkie's grief.
He recalled Jonse's threat against him. His father was
just like Jonse. His eyes went full and round. There it
was, the idea complete and full-blown in his mind. The
answer, the solution to everything. All this could be his
—the house, the land, everything. Then, he would have
to take no orders from anyone, and no one would dare
abuse him again. He used Quade once—the chuckle was
silent but very satisfying in his throat—why not use him
again? He would give the town a double reason for
wanting Quade's blood. Hobart would like that. Hobart
wanted all the reasons he could get to keep after Quade.
Wilkie solemnly nodded. He had nothing to fear from
Quade. Hobart would keep after him until he killed him
or ran him so far he wouldn't be big enough to make a
shadow.

He eased his gun from the holster. He said, "Paw,"
in a low voice.

M AcLENDON turned. He saw Wilkie's face and the
gun, and comprehension flashed into his eyes. But his
voice was calm enough. He said, "Wilkie. You're drunk.
Put that gun away."

Wilkie's lips twisted in a snarl. "Don't you be telling
me what to do. Jonse was always doing that. When it
got to the point where I couldn't stand it any longer—"

MacLendon's face went ashen, prompted by more
horror than fear. He said in a hoarse voice, "You killed
your brother. And blamed Quade."

Wilkie cackled. "Everybody believed it. Even you. They'll believe me again."

MacLendon was having difficulty with his breathing. He said in a choked voice, "Wilkie, I think you're a little crazy. Maybe I've known it a long time. I forgave you a lot of things, but not Jonse's death. God-damn you, Wilkie." His hand flung out toward the gun on the mantel.

Wilkie screamed, "Don't do that," and pulled the trigger.

MacLendon seemed to grow taller under the impact of the bullet. One hand clawed at his chest, and with the other, he still tried to reach the pistol.

Wilkie watched his father's terrible struggle in awed fascination. If he touched that gun, he was going to shoot him again, and his finger was tensing, when MacLendon's arm dropped.

MacLendon was sagging, and the knowledge of futility was in his eyes. His voice was little stronger than a whisper as he said again, "God-damn you, Wilkie. I wish I could kill you."

He fell abruptly, sprawling limply on the rug before the fireplace.

Wilkie stared at him and muttered. "You're never going to tell me what to do again." He cackled suddenly. It wasn't any use talking to the Colonel. The Colonel was dead.

Wilkie looked about the room, his eyes crafty. Now, which window did Quade shoot the Colonel from? He decided on the one on the left-hand side of the front door. Quade had sneaked up on the front porch, looked through the window, and then killed the Colonel from there.

Wilkie moved to the window and looked at the body. Yes, the Colonel was in line. Everything was perfect. An instant alarm flashed into his eyes as he thought of something. If Quade fired through the window, wouldn't the glass be broken? Wilkie cursed at his over-sight and broke the pane with a savage slash of his gun muzzle. He put the gun away and stared about the room. Everything looked right now—everything was perfect.

His laughter was harsh and metallic. All he had to do was to ride into town and tell Hobart and the rest of them what happened. He had no doubt of them believing him—they wanted to believe him. His face lighted, and he laughed again. He had run Quade off for the second time. He was building himself a mighty big standing in the town.

FOURTEEN

QUADE looked through the glasses again and frowned. Ten minutes ago, he had thought the approaching rider was Osley. Now, the man was close enough for him to be sure. From his vantage point of height in the foothills Quade swept the country on both sides of Osley. It was flat and open. Osley was riding alone. And he was riding with purpose as though he had a definite destination in mind.

Quade muttered, "He's riding after me. Only Priam knew where he was, and a quick suspicion flooded Quade's mind. He discarded the suspicion and swore. If Osley knew where Quade was from Priam, it would be because of no unfavorable reason to Quade. A few days on the dodge made a man jumpy and nervous. He remembered every word Osley had said the last time he talked to him, but still, he would take no foolish chances. There were too many intervening hours between then and now that Quade did not know about.

He swept the country with the glasses for a final time before he walked to his saddle. Osley was alone for certain. He pulled the carbine from its scabbard and went back to the big rock and lay down behind it. In twenty minutes, Osley should be within hailing distance. He ran the backs of his fingers across his beard and grunted irritably. It did not take long for a man to go damn near animal.

He watched Osley's progress, and the questions kept flooding his mind. What did Osley want; why was he riding out here? He grunted again and shifted his position. He would have to wait until Osley was here for his answers.

He saw Osley hesitate a moment at the lightning-struck pine, glance to his right, then quarter up the hill. Osley had his directions all right.

He waited until Osley was a hundred yards away, then called, "Osley." The flatness of his voice carried its warning.

Osley threw up his head at his name and called, "Hello, Quade." He never even hesitated his slow climb.

Quade sighed and laid down the carbine. Osley's actions were open. He meant what he said the other night.

He came around the big rock to meet Osley and growled, "You ride in here like there isn't a scare in you. I'm a wanted man."

Osley did not respond to his humor. He said soberly, "Make that double wanted, Quade. You killed the Colonel last night."

"I did?" Quade said and shook his head. "I could've sworn I was right out here."

Osley climbed stiffly down. He said morosely, "Damn all this trouble." He caught Quade's oblique glance, and his face reddened. "I ain't hollering about the trouble," he said testily. "I'm hollering cause I can't get a hold of it."

"Coffee's on the fire," Quade said and led the way to the pot, sitting among the dying embers. Wrangle nickered at the presence of another horse. Wrangle was lonely, too.

He poured Osley a cup and hunkered down on his heels. He would let Osley commence the talking.

Osley gulped the coffee down and said, "I needed that. I'm getting too old to be pounding a saddle."

"Priam told you where I was." Quade made it a statement.

Osley nodded. "You can't be letting him come out here anymore. If someone gets the idea what he's doing, he can be hurt bad. There's some wild people in that town."

Quade rolled a cigarette. This was going to make the problem of supplies more difficult. "How did I kill the Colonel?"

"You sneaked up to his porch window. You shot him from there."

"Did Wilkie report it?"

Osley nodded. "He rode into town after he drove you away."

Quade said dryly, "It seems like I'm scared to death of him. This makes him a big man. He owns everything."

Osley reached for the coffee-pot. There was half a cup left in it.

"You should've sent word you were coming," Quade said and grinned

"This is no joking matter," Osley said in a crabby voice. "Stobie's got two posses out. He's crazy to get you, Jim."

"The whole town believe it?" Quade asked.

"Most of them do." Osley's voice was weary. "I went out there last night, after Wilkie came in. The glass in the window was broken. The pieces of it were laying on the porch." His tone was bitter. "Wilkie wasn't even smart enough to break the glass so it fell the right way."

"Nobody else saw it?"

"They don't want to see it. A small town gets pretty dull, Jim. This is big excitement."

Quade nodded in understanding. The town had a name to hunt, and the excitement of the chase flogged them on. None of those people would want to stop and look at facts. "So Stobie's pushing hard," he said.

"Hard isn't the word for it," Osley said gloomily. "He's taken over my office. He's running things."

"You can fire him."

Osley sighed. "The only way I can do that is with a gun."

"And he's faster," Quade said softly.

"Yes." Osley's agreement was flat. "But that's my problem. You've got to get out of the country. They'll pick you up, if you stay around here. They'll make bigger and bigger sweeps. The damn fools almost shot Wade Stewart this morning. At a distance, he kinda looks like you. He had sense enough to stop and holler. But they're ready to turn on anything that even reminds them of you. They're watching the Chesbroughs, and they can hurt them."

Q UADE swore in a flat voice. Everything Osley said was true. But if left, Susan and Priam would be as bad off as when he first met them. The town's dislike would have to center around something, and the Chesbroughs were too handy. Wilkie would work out his old hatreds against them, and the town would not stop him. Quade recalled Wilkie's handling of Susan, and his eyes burned. He said, "I'm not leaving. Where's Wilkie now?"

Osley said, "You'd never get close to him. When I left, he was in town getting drunk. I know what you're thinking. But it'd never work. Wilkie's smart enough to stay around people. Even if you got him alone and beat an admission out of him, he'd deny it later."

"Not if several other people heard him."

Osley shook his head in exasperation. "They'd never let you even get started. If killing Wilkie would do you any good, I could even go along with that. But it won't. To get close to him, you'll probably have to kill some-one else. I wouldn't stand for that. I know they're after you, but they're acting in ignorance. I'd have to go after you then, Jim."

Quade looked at the stubborn set of Osley's face. The man meant it. And what Osley said was so. If he stayed around, sooner or later he would have to kill some over-zealous posseman—or be killed.

He said, "I'm not leaving."

Osley said hopelessly, "I figured you'd say that. What's the answer?"

Quade mulled it over in his mind. Every problem had its answer. Only the finding of it was difficult. Names poured into his brain. Priam and Susan, the Colonel and Wilkie. Jonse was his high-pitched, almost adolescent voice. His eyes lighted, and he leaned forward. "Osley, you know Hank Cameron, don't you?"

"The best saddle maker in the country," Osley said. "Who does he sound like?"

Osley frowned in concentration.

Quade said impatiently, "Doesn't he sound like Jonse?"

Osley said uncertainly, "Maybe." His frown faded. "Now that you mention it, I guess he does a little."

"Wilkie's going to have a lot eating on him," Quade said. "The whisky won't help it any. If I can trick him into saying what I want him to say—"

Osley frowned again. "You mean have Cameron's voice work on Wilkie's conscience? Oh hell. That's really shooting wild."

"It's all I've got left," Quade said. "I'm going in and talk to Hank tonight. If he'll help me, I'm going to try."

Osley said an explosive, "No. You can't go in there."

"I'm going. You can help me or stand aside."

Their eyes locked and held, and two stubborn wills warred against each other. Osley finally sighed and said, "I guess we haven't got anything else. I've talked to Sanders and Coniston. They don't go along with the rest of the town. Maybe we can work on Wilkie. But you stay here."

Quade shook his head. "Something could happen to Hank, I won't let him get hurt trying to help me."

Osley said, "Damnit. If you're seen in town, you'll have to shoot your way out. I'm warning you, if anybody's killed outside of Wilkie, I'll be against you just as quick as I'm for you." His sigh was long and weary. "All right. I'll meet you in Cameron's shop after midnight. Don't you move until I get there."

Quade's grin was tight. Osley stated his stand plainly enough. Doc Sanders was wrong, when he included Osley in his statement about the town. Osley didn't have the disease at all.

FIFTEEN

OSLEY put a sly glance on Cameron and said "There's some damned funny angles about those MacLendon killings."

Cameron was thinning a piece of leather. He laid the leather down but held the knife. He waved the knife in Osley's face and said furiously. "I swear to God, Burt Osley, if you ever had any brains, they've leaked out by now. Quade didn't have anything to do with killing Jonse or the Colonel. Any damn fool ought to be able to see that." He snorted in outrage. "Wilkie hated Jonse. Everybody knew that. They ride away together, and Wilkie comes back and says he drove Quade off. And he drives Quade off again, when he comes after the Colonel. You know Jim Quade. If he was after the MacLendons, do you think he would run from Wilkie?"

Osley was grinning, and the old man's rage increased. "Laugh at me, damn you. You know what I think? Wilkie killed Jonse, and somehow the Colonel found out about it. Wilkie had to kill him, too. Now, laugh your damned head off."

Osley said, "That's kind of the way I figure it, too."

His grin grew broader at the slack-jawed look in Cameron's face. "Had to find out how you felt about it, Hank."

Cameron sputtered indignantly. "Your office is running posses all over the county after Quade."

"Not my office, Osley said quietly. "Stobie is. The town's backing Stobie."

Cameron said in a questioning tone, "It'd be easier to join them, Burt."

A faint red touched Osley's cheeks at Cameron's reference to the earlier months. "Harder in the long run, Hank. The best way to handle trouble is to jump astraddle it, while it's forming. A man never broke no

128

horses by sitting in the shade and wishing they were broke. I've known it all along."

The judging went out of Cameron's voice. "Quade kind of reminded you of it."

"Yes," Osley said simply.

Cameron bobbed his head. "That hard son has that knack. He'd been good for this town, if we'd let him stay around."

"He's around, Hank."

Cameron leaned forward, his eyes bright. "I thought you didn't come in here for just some idle talk. What are you figuring on?"

"He needs some help, Hank. He's got a wild idea, and there might be something to it. But we've got to set it up for him."

Cameron's breathing came faster. "You got a piece of it for me?"

"The biggest," Osley said gravely. "It could be dangerous."

Cameron snorted. "You might've scared me a few years ago with that. I've lived a long time, and I've seen about everything. What do I do?"

Osley said, "Anybody ever mention you sound like Jonse MacLendon?"

Cameron was indignant. "They always put it that way. I came a long time before that pup did. Why didn't they say he sounded like me?"

Osley grinned, then his face sobered. "Wilkie's had a couple of nights for something to gnaw on him. He's spent most of those nights in the Orient trying to drown something. If a man shot his father and brother, he's going to think about it."

Cameron cackled with delight. "I get it. If he thinks he hears Jonse's voice coming at him out of the night, it might scare hell out of him. It might scare him enough so that he'd yell out against that voice. Is that it?"

Osley nodded. "That's it, Hank."

Cameron slapped his thigh. "Hell yes, it could work, Burt. At night, a man gets to thinking of all the things he's done wrong. They look bigger and closer to him then." He pursed his lips and shook his head. "Wilkie's got to be by himself, if we're going to work on him. How you going to get him out of the saloon?"

"I'm going to work on it now," Osley said and stood. He put reflective eyes on Cameron. "I wanted Quade to let us handle it. But he insists on coming in. He'll be here about midnight. He's going with you, Hank, to see that nothing happens to you."

"I got nothing to worry about then. But he's taking a hell of a chance, Burt."

"A big chance," Osley agreed and went out the door.

He moved down the darkened street, his mind busy. He had a couple of hours until midnight. It was enough time but not a fat margin by any means. He had to clear the way as much as possible for Quade, and that meant getting Stobie and a few of the others out of town.

He stopped in at his office, and Hobart sat at Osley's desk, his boot heels propped up on it. He scowled at the ceiling, and Osley knew frustration was gnawing on him.

Hobart looked at him. He did not remove his heels, nor make any attempt to get up. In Hobart's mind, the change-over was already made.

Osley hoped he put the right note of excitement in his voice. He said, "Stobie. Howell just told me Quade was at his place not an hour ago. Quade held a gun on him and stripped him of supplies."

Hobart's eyes grew hard and bright. He uttered an oath and jumped to his feet. He reached for his gun-belt and was buckling it on, when he stopped, his eyes going suspicious.

"How come you're telling me?"

Osley said earnestly, "I want to go with you, Stobie."

The suspicion left Hobart's face, and he said triumphantly, "So that's it. No, you don't. You see you're wrong and want to be in on the finish. You think that will make people forget how you sat around."

Osley muttered, "A posse wouldn't follow me, Stobie."

"Hell no," Hobart said in vicious agreement. "No one would follow you. You're through." He eyed the star on Osley's vest, a covetous shine in his eyes. "You're trying to hang onto a job that's already slipped through your hands. Where's Howell now?"

Osley said, "Stobie." He held out a hand in supplication. He let the hand fall as he saw no relenting in

Hobart's face. His sigh was long and mournful as he said, "I've been a damned fool, Stobie."

"You have," Hobart said crisply, "Where's Howell?"

Osley stared at the floor. He hoped he looked like a beaten man. "I don't know. I talked to him in front of the bank. Stobie, let me ride with you?"

Hobart's teeth flashed in a wicked grin. "You haven't got a chance," he said and went out the door.

Osley moved to the door and watched Hobart rush down the street. Stobie would not find Howell, and Osley doubted he would look for him very long. This was the first report on Quade in several days, and Hobart would waste no time in acting upon it.

"Stobie," Osley said softly. "I hope you wear your ass out tonight." He was kind of proud of that piece of acting. He had not known it was in him.

He stayed in the office doorway until the posse clattered out of town. At this hour, Hobart had trouble rounding up a large number of men. He took six with him, but that many would help. It was seven less triggers against Quade, when he came into town.

He went down the walk, his face thoughtful. There was more setting-up ahead of him, and it was important. He swore softly. Every phase of it was important, and when he thought of how every detail had to dovetail it scared him. He met Coniston and Sanders outside the Orient, and Sanders said, "Wilkie's inside. I don't see how he holds that much whisky."

"Maybe the whisky will work for us," Osley said. He looked at Coniston and asked, "Sure you know what to do?"

Coniston nodded and smiled faintly. "It's a crazy thing, Burt. But little enough to do for Quade."

Osley said, "It's not crazy if it gets Wilkie out of here. Not if it puts a thought into his head. Come inside in about five minutes."

He walked into the Orient with Sanders. There were only four men in the place, and Wilkie was one of them. He sat at the rear table, his eyes glassy. A half-empty whisky bottle sat before him, and as Osley looked at him, Wilkie reached for the bottle and drank directly from it. His hand shook, and some of the whisky trickled down his chin. He had not shaved for several days, and he looked bad.

Sanders stepped to the bar with Osley. He put a side glance on Wilkie and said softly, "There's a picture of remorse."

Osley doubted it was remorse; he doubted Wilkie was that sensitive, but something was eating on him.

Sanders ordered a bottle of sarsaparilla, and at Osley's look of surprise smiled faintly. He said quietly, "I found I didn't need the other as much as I thought I did, Burt." His eyes were far away, digging up some old scene out of the past. "I was scared of my first operation, and I did some drinking before it. I botched that operation, Burt, and I've carried it with me ever since. I've ran scared for a lot of years, and found I didn't have to." He looked directly at Osley and said, "Quade taught me that. He's quite a teacher."

Osley said abruptly, "Yes." It was all summed up in the one word.

The five minutes seemed to take forever to pass. Wilkie finished most of the remaining whisky in the period. Osley kept watching him. Wilkie looked like he was running scared. Was he running scared enough? That was the big question.

Coniston rushed into the room, his face agitated. He ordered a drink, and his hand shook as he raised it to his lips.

Osley judiciously watched him. Coniston was doing a fair job.

"I needed that," Coniston said. "My God, how I needed that." His word drew every eye toward him, and Coniston said, "Do you know who I just saw?"

He paused for effect, and Osley growled a mental, "Don't overdo it."

Coniston said huskily, "I just saw Jonse MacLendon."

It filled eyes with surprise and slackened mouths. It reached through the whisky fog in Wilkie's mind, and Osley saw him go rigid.

It took a few seconds for the words to work on Wilkie's mind, then he jumped to his feet, spilling his chair over backward. "You're crazy," he bellowed. "Jonse is dead."

Coniston wiped his forehead. "I thought so, too," he

said in a shaky voice. "But I saw him. Not fifty yards from me. He looked like he was hunting for something."

Wilkie rushed toward him, and Osley tensed thinking. Wilkie intended harm to Coniston. Wilkie stopped abruptly a couple of feet from him and thrust his face almost up against Coniston's.

"You're crazy," he yelled as though sheer volume of sound could sweep away Coniston's words.

Coniston recoiled from him, and Osley guessed Wilkie's breath was strong.

Wilkie turned his head toward Sanders. "Doc, tell him he's crazy. You've got a crazy man on your hands."

Sanders' face was grave. "I don't know, Wilkie. Do the dead return? That's an often argued question."

Denial broke out all over the room, and Sanders raised a hand to quell it.

Coniston said stubbornly, "I know what I saw."

Sanders said, "There's been reported instances of the dead being seen before." The denials rose again, and he said in a challenging tone, "You don't believe me. Come to my office. I'll give you a dozen books with accounts of it."

The denials weakened. If this was in books, it carried the ring of authority. Doc Sanders said it was so, and Doc Sanders was an educated man.

Osley looked at Wilkie. Wilkie was pop-eyed, and there was no color in his face. He was having trouble with his breathing, and he had to try several times before the words would come.

"You're all a pack of God-damned fools," he screeched. "Jonse is dead. He's going to stay that way. Give me a bottle," he yelled at the bartender.

He grabbed the bottle from the man's hand and weaved out of the room.

Osley heard someone say, "Poor Wilkie's taking Jonse's death hard."

Osley's eyes were cold. That was the way he wanted Wilkie to take it.

He followed Wilkie outside. Behind him, he heard fresh argument going on. That argument would hold them for hours. He had to admit that Coniston and Sanders did a job. He grinned faintly. Almost as good as the one he turned in.

He followed Wilkie to the Parker House. He waited outside until he saw a light go on in the second-floor room. He saw the blind jerked down before he turned away. Pulling that blind would shut off no thoughts. He hoped they were eating on Wilkie with long, savage teeth.

He turned toward Cameron's shop. It was pretty close to midnight, and he had done everything he could do. Wilkie was by himself, and he had a mind full of thoughts.

SIXTEEN

THE TOWN was dark, the street deserted. The only spot of light along the entire street came from the Orient Saloon, and it seemed wan and dispirited, fading before it fully washed across the walk. Quade stood pressed against a building at the end of the street, his eyes searching every shadow, his ears attuned for the least unusual sound. Wrangle was tethered a half mile behind him, and Quade had felt terribly naked and vulnerable during that walk. He knew the hue and cry that would follow the first pair of eyes that saw him, and a man on foot was so helpless, when it came to flight. But horseman ran a much greater risk of being seen than a sulking shadow close to the ground. A man had to weigh one risk against another and take the lesser one. He thought wryly, it seemed that every move a man took carried its attendant risks. The only way he could avoid all of them was not to live.

His nerves were stretched tight as his eyes probed the street. Each forward step would increase in danger, for any man seeing him would try to stop him, and he would not be stopped. He respected Osley for his warning, but it did not change things—it only complicated them.

Cameron's shop was four doors away, and Quade thought he had better try the rear door. He moved to the alley, running behind the buildings. It was blacker here, and a sense of instinctive feeling was more important than his eyes. A tin can turned under his boot and rolled away with a hollow clang, and it sounded loud enough to wake up the entire town. He remained motionless, his heart clogging his breathing until he was certain no one but himself heard the noise. He moved a dozen feet farther, and a small, dark form streaked across the alley. He jumped and his hand grabbed at his gun. He swore and shook his head. That was only a cat. He was stretched too tight, and the tightness made him jumpy, but what else could be expected of

135

a man, in a town, where almost every pair of hands was against him. He was not even sure of Hank Cameron. The old man had expressed dislike for Jonse, and that dislike had included the whole tribe of MacLendons, but did it still stand in the face of what had happened? He would not know until he talked to him.

He counted off the back doors, and if he had not missed one in the darkness, this was the rear of Cameron's shop. Quade hesitated before he knocked. Was there a sleeping room in the rear of the shop, or did the old man have his quarters somewhere else? Quade cursed himself. It was something he should have found out.

He knocked softly, and the sound seemed to roll along the alley. If the old man was a hard sleeper, that would never awaken him.

He was debating upon applying more pressure, when the door opened so suddenly it startled him.

Hank Cameron said, "Get in here. You trying to wake up the whole town?"

A sigh eased some of Quade's tension. Osley must have talked to Cameron, for the old man was expecting him.

Quade felt more secure, when the door closed behind him. He heard the sounds of Cameron's movement, then the light of a lamp drove the shadows into the corners of the room.

"Nobody can see in here," Cameron said gruffly.

In the lamp-light, he looked owl-eyed and waiting, and Quade said, "Hank, I need your help. I didn't kill either Jonse or the Colonel."

Cameron snorted. "Any damn fool ought to be able to see that." He cackled at Quade's expression. "Osley's been working on this. He said for you to wait here until he gets here. He ought to be along any minute." He scowled at Quade. "Did you think there was no appreciation in anybody in this town?"

At the moment, Quade could not trust himself to speak. A man sat out by himself and imagined himself without friends. The realization of how wrong he could be made him go soft inside.

Cameron said, "I know what I'm going to try to do. If it doesn't work, at least, we'll scare hell out of Wilkie."

Quade said, "It's got to work, Hank." He wanted this town to be his; he never wanted to move again. He wanted Susan and all the rest of it that went to build up a bright picture of the future.

"We got a chance," Cameron said. He turned his head at the knock on the front door. "That'll be Osley," he said.

Quade moved to the front of the shop with Cameron, and Cameron eased the door open a crack. "Burt," he said and threw the door wide. "How'd it go?"

Osley stepped inside. He said, "Hello, Jim. Better than I hoped for. He's in his room. It's on the second floor, the north corner room. His light was still on, when I left a few minutes ago. The hotel porch roof is right below his window. If you can get up on that, you'd be on a level with his window. I don't know how you're going to get any closer to him." He gloomily shook his head. He was scared inside. It had gone along all right so far, but one little slip, and the whole thing was shot. So many little things could happen that a man could not foresee. "If anybody sees you on that roof, they'd shoot you off like a pigeon." He swung his eyes toward Cameron. "They'll shoot you just as quick because you're with him."

Cameron snorted. "You can't talk me out of it."

Osley was not trying to talk him out of anything; he was just pointing out the obvious.

Cameron said, "Nobody's going to see us this hour of the night."

Osley sighed. He hoped Cameron was right. He had done as much as he could. A man made his plans, then he had to stick by them.

Quade said, "One thing bothers me. If we scare Wilkie into saying anything, will the town believe Hank?"

Osley said, "Coniston and Doc Sanders will be with me outside his door. That makes four of us to hear anything he might say."

Quade's voice was gruff. "That should do it." He wanted to say a 'thanks' but he was afraid it would come out all wrong.

Osley's eyes were intent on Quade's face. "I want this to work. For you—for me." He tried to grin, and it came off twisted. "If it doesn't, we'll all be running."

It would take timing and a lot of luck. If a man thought about all the 'ifs' involved, it could drive him crazy. Quade tried to say lightly, "A man makes his bet. Then he either has the cards, or he doesn't."

Osley glared at Cameron before he left the shop. "You make it good, you understand?"

Cameron said shrilly, "You take care of what you're supposed to do. Don't be fretting none about me."

He's looking forward to this with only excitement, Quade thought. There's no fear in him. Maybe it was that way with the old. Perhaps the long years of living had taught them that most of the fears were only spectres.

"We'll be ready by the time you get there," Osley said and slipped out the front door.

Cameron turned bright eyes toward Quade. "What do you want me to say?"

"Whatever comes into your head. Whatever you think might drive Wilkie into talking."

The old man said gloatingly, "I'll drive him. I'll torture him good."

In spite of his bleak thoughts, Quade laughed. He placed a hand on Cameron's shoulder and said, "I think you will."

SEVENTEEN

CAMERON went out the door first. He whispered back, "All clear," and Quade stepped out onto the walk. From now on, luck held them in her palm, and Quade knew how capricious the lady could be. She could keep her fingers bent protectively about them, or she could fling them out for anybody to see.

The hotel was two blocks down the street, and the two used every shadow in reaching it. The night was cool, but still, Quade found himself bathed in sweat. Tight nerves could bring out as much sweat as muscular exertion. A dog yapped suddenly, and Quade's heart was a ball, leaping into his throat and blocking his breathing. Then he realized the barking was not at them—it came from the next street over. He heard Cameron's soft cursing and thought there was a shake in his voice. He touched Cameron's shoulder, and the old man threw off his hand. Cameron was tense, not fearful.

They stood across the street from the hotel. There was a single light in the building, coming from a second-story, corner window above the pillar-supported porch, that covered the hotel's segment of the walk. Wilkie's room, Osley said.

The porch roof could be reached my shinnying up one of the pillars, and Quade looked doubtfully at Cameron.

The old man guessed his doubts and said crankily, "I can climb it as good as you."

Quade drew a breath and boldly crossed the street. The few seconds during the climbing to the roof would be bad. But once they reached it, they would know a comparative safety, for few men ever glanced above their head-height.

Cameron's words were stronger than his action. He wrapped his arms and legs about the post, he struggled and wriggled, but he made little upward progress. He seemed to make an agonizing amount of noise, and

Quade resisted the temptation to glance fearfully about him. He bent low, got his shoulders under Cameron's butt and straightened under the old man's weight. Cameron stood, and his boot heels dug into Quade's shoulders. He wobbled back and forth, shifting his feet to keep his balance, and Quade hissed, "Stand still."

A boot heel scraped Quade's ear, and he said a silent curse against the burn of it. He straightened to his full height, and pushed Cameron over the edge of the porch. He saw it sag under the old man's weight, and that was another worry. Would it hold under their combined weight. He added this risk to all the others as he glanced about him.

The noise, Cameron made getting onto the roof, did not seem to disturb anyone. No lights were flashing on in the buildings, and the street was still empty. He looked up, and Cameron's face peered at him from over the edge of the roof. The old man extended a hand, and Quade shook his head. He could make it better alone.

He shinnied up a pillar and pulled himself over the edge. The porch roof was made of metal, and Quade muttered an oath as a bent-up edge of tin gouged a chunk out of the heel of his palm.

He lay there, sucking on the wound as he sized up what was ahead of them. They were eight feet from the window, eight feet of sloping, rattling surface. And vulnerable again, for if Wilkie heard them and came to the window, they would be in full view of him. Quade drew his gun. If Wilkie came to the window, he would have to shoot him to protect the old man.

Cameron started to get to his feet, and Quade drew him back down. Crawling would be less noisy. The metal surface would be a vast resounding board for a boot heel.

The roof shook and rattled up as they moved up it. It seemed to Quade it was a great drum and each stroke announced their presence. At any second, he expected to see the blind at the window fly up. He reached the window and cautiously stood, pressing tight against the building beside it. He motioned Cameron to do the same on the other side and gestured him silent as he listened.

The window was open, and the night breeze rattled

and flapped the cracked green blind. Quade heard nothing from the room, and those torturing questions commenced again. Suppose Wilkie had gone out, suppose Osley was mistaken, and this was not even Wilkie's room. Then he heard a man's voice coming from within the room, and for an instant, thought the man was talking to someone. Then he realized the man was carrying on a monologue such as a drunk might do, for the muttering voice went on and on, not pausing as it would do, if it were in conversation. That answered the question of the room's occupancy. It had to be Wilkie. Quade thought, we could not have gone this far and have it be otherwise.

He motioned to Cameron, and the old man said in a hollow voice, "Wilkie." He let the name trail off on a sighing note.

To Quade, it had an errie effect, an effect that touched his skin with icy little fingers. It sounded like Jonse's voice, it had all the nuances. How it would sound to a drunken, guilt-ridden man was another matter.

The muttering in the room stopped, and Quade could almost feel the stiffening that seized the man behind the blind. He motioned at Cameron again.

"Wilkie," Cameron said again. "Are you hearing me, Wilkie?"

Quade heard the rush of feet toward the window. He pressed as tightly as he could against the wall and saw Cameron trying to make himself as flat as possible.

The roller whirred as the blind flew up, and Quade scarcely dared breathe. If Wilkie looked to either side, he could not help but see them. Quade had to depend upon the night's cloak and the hope that Wilkie would only look for something directly before him. It seemed that Wilkie stayed at the window forever before Quade heard the slow retreat of his footsteps.

"There's nothing out there," Wilkie muttered, and Quade caught the desperate need in the man's voice to convince himself.

"Yes, there is," the hollow voice said. "And you know who it is. You thought you killed me, didn't you, Wilkie?"

Wilkie made a sound that was half sob and half scream. "Damn you, Jonse," he whimpered. "Damn you."

The voice relentlessly continued. "You killed Paw, too, didn't you? I saw it."

"You didn't," Wilkie denied shrilly. "Nobody was there."

"I was there," the hollow voice said. "I'm always going to be with you. Whatever you do, Wilkie, I'm always going to be right beside you."

The pure terror in Wilkie's scream sent chilling ripples along Quade's skin. A man had to be in torment to scream so.

"Damn you, Jonse," Wilkie sobbed. "You're dead. I killed you once. I can kill you again."

T HE blast of the shot made Quade twitch. He heard the slug rip through the blind. Wilkie could see nothing, but that did not stop him from shooting. He fired almost as fast as he could pull the trigger. He screamed at the top of his voice as he fired, and Quade doubted that the man was even trying to form words.

The slugs tore through the blind, and Quade heard their impact as they buried into the wooden buildings across the street. He counted five shots and still, he hesitated. Did Wilkie carry five or six loads in his gun? He thought it must be only five, for terror was pulling that trigger, and a sixth load would have been fired as readily as the others.

He raised an edge of the blind and peeked into the room. Wilkie was thumbing fresh loads into his gun. Quade tore the blind from its roller and climbed through the window. He yelled, "Drop it, Wilkie."

Wilkie stood in the center of the room, weaving back and forth. His hair was down in his eyes, and streams of saliva ran down from his lip corners. He raised his head and stared at Quade, and his eyes were those of a madman's. Neither Quade's words, nor the sight of the gun Quade held had any effect upon him. He dropped a shell in his feverish haste and put another into the cylinder. "Damn you, Jonse," he snarled. "You're never going to get me."

"Wilkie," Quade shouted.

Wilkie was raising his gun, and Quade realized no words could ever reach into that terrorized mind. Nothing short of a bullet could stop him.

He pulled the trigger and saw the impact of the bullet knock Wilkie backward. Wilkie's arms flew up, and his gun arced across the room, landing near a corner. He went backward in a series of short, broken steps, his weight coming down jarringly on his boot-heels. He half spun, then collapsed, landing on his side. He rolled over on his back, his glazing eyes staring up at Quade. He tried to speak, and saliva and the rush of blood choked off his words. He half lifted his head, then it fell back with a small thud, and the light went out of his eyes.

Quade shook his head, knowing almost a pity for him. In those few seconds of terror, Wilkie had known all the hell a man should know.

He heard cries from the street outside and hurried to the window. Lights were coming on up and down the street, and across it, a door opened, and the dark figure of a man appeared framed in it. Quade pulled Cameron in through the window. The knocking on the door could wait a moment. The volume of cries from the street was swelling as men rushed up and down it. Those shots had jerked most of them from a sound sleep, and their judgment would be as faulty as their tempers were thin. He heard an indiscriminate shot from out there and almost nodded. They were ready to fire at anything that moved. The porch roof would not be safe for even a cat.

The pounding on the door increased, and he crossed to it. "Quade," he heard Osley call. "What's happening?"

He opened the door, and the tight lines in Osley's face melted at the sight of him. He stepped into the room and asked, "Did it go all right?"

Sanders and Coniston crowded in after him, and Quade said unnecessarily. "Wilkie's dead," for all of them were staring at Wilkie's body.

Cameron said in a gloating voice, "I did it real well, didn't I?"

Quade said in a weary voice, "Stop it, Hank." It was done and over, and he wanted to forget it as soon as possible.

He looked at Osley and asked, "You heard?"

"All of it," Osley muttered, and Sanders and Coniston nodded in agreement.

Coniston smiled faintly at Quade. "It was something we already knew, but hearing him say it makes it better." He looked at the body, and a shudder ran through him.

Quade knew what he was trying to say. Now, the last feeble doubt was washed away.

Sanders said, "The last of the MacLendons. The whisky made the tortured moments in his mind real." His attempt at a smile was a small, wry movement of his lips. "If I am ever tempted to reach for a drink again, I hope I remember Wilkie."

Quade looked from face to face. It was a sobering moment for all of them. For each man was casting back and remembering and not liking what he dredged up in his thoughts. A dead man was so powerless, and yet at one time, all of them had walked in fear of this one and the others, who bore the name MacLendon.

Osley said abruptly, "Don't leave the hotel, Quade. The town will be stirred up tonight. It will take a lot of explaining to calm it down. You and Hank sleep here. In the morning, it will be different."

His tone could have carried more conviction, and Quade wondered about it. He supposed some of the hot-heads would be hard to convince, and that was worrying Osley. But with the town's doctor and banker backing Osley's story, it should carry the necessary weight. Quade pushed it from his mind. He was too tired to think much about it now. He did not even mind if Cameron snored. Nothing could reach through the weight of weariness he carried.

EIGHTEEN

HOBART paced the floor of the office. His eyes were wild. The morning's heat had pushed into the office. That and his inner emotions were wringing sweat out of him, dampening his shirt. He stopped and turned his head toward Osley, and his face was ugly.

Osley watched him with a detached curiosity. Hobart acted like a man on the brink of losing something he thought well within his grasp, a man who was determined his fingers would not be pried loose. There was anger in Osley and an admitted honest fear. Words would not stop Hobart, for Osley had tried his best. That left one other thing, and Osley's mind shied from touching it.

"You tricked me last night," Hobart said, and there was a sort of frenzy in his voice.

For an instant, Osley thought that frenzy would drive him beyond restraint, and he tensed.

"I'll remember that," Hobart said. "You're all a bunch of liars. Do you think I'd believe any of you?"

"Then you're the only man in town, who doesn't," Osley said.

"You got together with Sanders and Coniston and cooked up this story," Hobart accused.

"There's Cameron, too," Osley pointed out.

Hobart made a sharp gesture with his hand, dismissing Cameron with the others. "You were afraid of Quade from the first minute he rode into town. Don't try to lie out of it. I saw it."

Osley thought wryly, I was afraid, Stobie. Not the way you thought. But I was afraid, Now, I'm afraid in a different direction.

Hobart stabbed a finger at Osley's face. "Quade killed the MacLendons. And by God, he's going to pay for it."

"You don't believe that, Stobie."

"I believe it," Hobart snapped.

Maybe he did, Osley thought. Maybe Hobart could

not unmake his mind without finding too many weaknesses in himself. A guilty Quade meant so many things to Stobie Hobart—it meant standing with the town, it meant a secure hold on power that had almost been within his grasp.

Osley said hopelessly, "You're wrong, Stobie. If you'll talk to Coniston or Sanders—"

"I'll talk to no one," Hobart snarled. "And I don't need you or your damned badge to back me up." He wrenched at the badge on his shirt. It came away with a small tearing sound, and a strip of the shirt's material was attached to it. He threw it on the floor at Osley's feet and yelled, "Take the damned thing."

Osley slowly stood. His mind no longer shied away from the thing he had to do. He had tried to find another road, and there was none to be found. He thought with a mournful quality, some things were like that. The fear was still in him, but it was not as bad as he thought it would be. He guessed most fear was like that. Once, a man faced up to it, it lost a great deal of its size.

He said, "Don't leave this office, Stobie."

Hobart bared his teeth in a mocking grin. "You think you can stop me."

"I can try," Osley said gravely.

He thought he was beat before he made the try, but he was going ahead, anyway. He thought with bleak humor, this was Jim Quade's fault. Quade had changed a lot of thinking in this town.

He made a grab for his gun and had not tugged it free of the holster before Hobart's gun was out and covering him.

"I ought to kill you," Hobart said. He stood on braced legs, his upper body bent, the heat in his eyes almost an insanity. "You've earned it." He sounded as though he were tasting the thought and finding it savory.

Osley sighed and let his hand fall away. He had never seen a draw more smooth nor fast. The only thing he could accomplish now by pushing harder against Hobart was a bullet in his belly. He had taken the big risk as it was, and suddenly sweat popped out on his face.

He said in a dull voice, "You're all wrong, Stobie."

HOBART laughed and put away his gun. "You're scared for Quade, aren't you? You just saw I can beat him. You tell him I'm going to kill him. In town or out. Wherever I find him. With or without him wearing a gun. I don't give a damn."

He sauntered to the door and looked at Osley with those wild, bright eyes. "You tell him that, sheriff, the next time you see him."

Then he was gone, and the echo of his steps down the walk seemed to hang in the air for a long time.

Osley shook his head, a slow, hopeless gesture. He reached for his hat and settled it firmly on his head. He was suddenly very tired and curiously empty of all emotion. He guessed the acceptance of the inevitable put that emptiness in him. This had been forming for a long time, from the moment Hobart first learned Quade was in town, and Osley knew nothing could have really changed its course. It might have been diverted for a little while, but the end was written with heavy, indelible strokes. Hobart made one correct statement. Osley was scared for Jim Quade.

He went out of the office and down the walk with heavy strides. How very well he knew both men involved. Neither of them could be turned from the coming moment. And each in his own mind felt justified as to the motives he had. That was the hell of it. Osley wondered how you could ever put people together and still have peace.

He knocked on the door of Quade's room and frowned at the answering silence. Had Quade gone out this early? He rattled the door-knob and shouted. "Quade. Quade."

He heard the stir in the room and knew relief. Quade would at least have his warning.

The door opened, and he saw the evidence of heavy sleep still on Quade's face. Any irritation Quade felt was swept away by Osley's expression.

Quade asked, "What is it?" and a knowledge of some kind was already building a tension in his voice.

Osley said, "Stobie's gone wild. He's after you, Jim."

"Ah," Quade said. Neither his face nor voice showed any surprise. He said, "Come in," and threw the door wide.

Hank Cameron was still in bed, and Quade said. "Let him sleep." He wore jeans over light summer underwear, and he crossed to the wash-stand on bare feet. He poured water into the basin and sloshed it onto his face. He absently wiped his face, and Osley noticed all his movements had the same quality as though his thoughts were miles away. The heavy, bemused touch of sleep was gone from his face, when he turned to look at Osley.

"Tell me about it," he said quietly. He tugged on his boots and buttoned his shirt as he listened.

Osley briefly described the scene with Hobart. "He won't quit, Jim," he said. "Stobie staked everything on the belief you were guilty. It made him a big man for a moment. He won't let go of it now."

Quade remembered the bright challenge in Hobart's eyes he had seen the first time they met. It did not make any difference what the reason was as long as Hobart had one that satisfied him.

"You're not going to leave," Osley said. There was not even an inflection of a question in his tone.

Quade thought of Susan, of the boy, of Priam, and each of them meant something to him. A man's roots burrowed deep without him fully realizing what was happening. He said in a matter-of-fact voice, "No. I'm not leaving."

Osley sighed. "I didn't think you would." He felt no argument at Quade's answer. Quade had earned his right to whatever he wanted. He said, "Then you'll have to kill him. He'll never let you rest."

Quade said softly, "I knew that sometime ago." The knowledge had been formed in the first brief contact with Hobart. If Jim Quade stayed around this town long, he would have to kill him.

He buckled on his gun-belt, and Osley's breathing sounded a little ragged.

Osley said, "I've never seen him faster than he was this morning. I never—" He stopped abruptly, realizing what he was saying.

A crooked smile moved Quade's lips. "You tried to stop him?" He did not need Osley's yes—it was written in his face.

Quade moved to him and briefly touched his shoulder. "Why, you damned fool," he said softly. "He might've killed you." A few weeks ago, he would have denied any possibility of it, but it was here—a growing feeling toward this man, toward the town. People made mistakes, and a man forgave them. The roots were longer than he suspected.

"I had to try," Osley said gruffly. He could blame that on Quade, too. A short while ago, and he would have approached it differently, he would approached it with personal safety as his prime motive.

"How's the town feel about it?" Quade asked.

"People are pretty damned ashamed of themselves."

"They needn't be," Quade said. Information was important to him. There was a softness in his face Osley had never seen before.

Quade moved to the door, and Osley said earnestly, "Be careful, Jim."

The heavy lines were back in Quade's face, and his eyes were dark and brooding. "I wish it wasn't necessary," he said and opened the door. He meant that. He wished he would never again buckle on his gun. The hooks of the past were worse than fish-hooks. Once they sank into a man he rarely got them out.

He went down into the hot, dusty street, stopping methodically at each likely place. In two of them, Hobart had been there a few moments ago. Quade knew the man would not leave town—not until this meeting was over. Hobart might step out of the next doorway, or he might be just around the next corner. It kept a man's nerves cruelly stretched, though nothing showed on Quade's face. Always before he had known a fatalistic acceptance that had been an armor, but that was gone in the steadily rising rebellion. He kept thinking of Susan and their future, and the rebellion would not be stopped. He found he was inwardly shaking, and that was not good.

In each place, Quade left word for Hobart that he was looking for him. Mowbry, the shoemaker, said fiercely, "I hope you blow his damned head off," and Coniston and Sanders came up to him and said, "Quade, we can stop this. We can run him out of town for you."

The warmth he felt at their words did not show on his face. He said, "It wouldn't do any good. He'd only be waiting for me someplace else." Such a move would strengthen Hobart's confidence—he would see it that

Quade was afraid and needed help. It would not weaken his purpose. He would only redouble his efforts to meet Quade someplace else.

Sanders said softly, "I guess some things have to be faced. You've taught us quite a bit about that. Luck, man," he said, his voice suddenly harsh.

CONISTON gripped Quade's hand hard, then both of them stepped back to the walk and let him go. Outwardly, Quade's face was as hard as ever, but he could feel the melting going on beneath the surface. This was his town and his people, and suddenly the lonely feeling was gone. The nervous inward trembling was gone, too, and he said a soft "Hell" in wonder.

He made the length of the main business street, then turned and came back. The sun was high enough so that it made no difference in which direction he walked. He could feel its heat through his clothing, and a faint film of sweat was already dampening his body. He kept flexing his fingers as he walked. Was this the last one? Did a man's past have to engulf his future? He knew a sudden wild rage at the bank wall the questions built and forced himself calm. He could see no further ahead than this coming moment, but he knew one thing for certain—he had everything to gain and everything on his side. A man could ask no more guarantee than that.

He was half-way down the street, when he saw the figure come out from a store and step off the walk. He sighed softly. The moment was here.

Nothing showed in his face and nothing broke that slow, measured walk. The street was empty except for the two men, though Quade was aware of the faces that peered out from doorways and windows.

Hobart came toward him in that same deliberate way, and when they were thirty feet apart, both men stopped as though by mutual consent.

"I'm right surprised," Hobart drawled. "I thought you'd be running by now. Or didn't Osley find you to warn you?"

"He found me," Quade said in a flat voice. "And you didn't think I'd be running."

Hobart thumbed his hat to the back of his head. From his face he might have been engaged in pleasant conversation. "You'd been smart, if you'd run."

The bright hunger was in his eyes, and the expression on his face fooled no one. He tasted deep of this moment, rolling it around in his head, before he pushed it to conclusion.

Quade knew it was useless, but he made one more try. "I've got no quarrel with you, Stobie."

Hobart's eyes gleamed. "You begging, Quade?"

Quade's eyes turned more frosty. A man wasted his breath in trying to reason with someone like Hobart. "You stupid bastard," he said. "You've been hunting for an excuse for this, ever since you saw me. I'm ready anytime you are."

Hobart's face turned a dull red. "I'm going to enjoy this," he growled.

Quade watched his eyes. The decision would break there before it showed in any muscle movement.

Hobart suddenly yelled, then grabbed for his gun. The yell was an old trick, supposed to be disconcerting. The flicker of emotion in Hobart's eyes put Quade to digging for his gun. He was smooth and fast, and his natural talent and experience were in the draw. He thought it was the fastest he had ever made, and he needed it. Hobart's gun was out and leveled before Quade pulled the trigger, and the two reports sounded as one. But Hobart's shot was knocked off course by the bullet plowing into his chest. It pocked the dust between Quade's feet, and Quade had been the fastest by the tiniest tick of time.

Hobart was hard hit. His mouth was slack with shock, and his eyes were filled with disbelief. Quade did not shoot again, even though Hobart still held onto his gun. But the gun hand was sagging, and the effort to lift an arm suddenly grown heavy brought out beads of sweat on Hobart's forehead. The man had tremendous animal vitality, or he could not have stayed upright as long as he did. He fought his fading muscle power with an intensity that sickened Quade. An ankle turned under him, almost throwing him, and he lurched in a series of broken steps before he regained his balance. There was no pain on his face, only that disbelief. He kept staring at Quade, and Quade knew the man looked at a moment of failure and was unprepared for it.

The sickness grew in Quade. Damn the eternal challenge that was in men like this one.

Hobart dropped his gun. He looked at his open hand, then raised his eyes to Quade's face. His lips were flecked with red, and his face was twisted as though he were crying. Maybe he is, Quade thought. A man could not be blamed for inwardly crying, when he saw with agonizing clarity the foolish waste of his course.

Hobart's knees buckled, and his arms flung up. He spun in a half circle and crashed into the dust. His right arm bounced up, then flopped back with a lifelessness that needed no doctor's confirmation.

Quade stared at him a long moment before he holstered his gun. The familiar bitterness was in his mouth, and he knew from experience the long days it would take before the taste passed. He turned and plodded down the street. People were coming out onto the walks. He prayed none of them would stop him and say the banal things that popped into people's heads in moments like these.

EPILOGUE

OSLEY set his chair in the early spring sun, sat down, leaned back against the wall, and sighed with pure animal contentment. He unfolded his paper, then laid it across his lap. He felt no real inclination to read. He just wanted to sit here and soak up this sunshine. "Damned winter," he growled. "Thought it'd never end." A man's bones must grow spongy as he aged. He knew his bones seemed to absorb a lot more than they used to.

He glanced up and down the street, and his sense of contentment grew. People were stirring lazily about, making only a pretense of working. He grinned as he watched Hamilton take fifteen minutes to open a box, a good two or three minute job at least. This was no day to be working; this was a day to sit and enjoy just being alive.

It was a good town—quiet and peaceful, the people of it having a liking and respect for each other—the way a town should be. It was odd how a remark someone said stuck in one's mind. It was eight months ago that Doc Sanders said this town was suffering from bankruptcy of principle. He could not say it now; he would not even want to. Doc was different these days. He acted as though he might even like himself a little. We're all different, Osley thought soberly.

He turned his head at the rumble of wagon wheels down the street, and his face brightened at the sight of Quade and Susan. If Quade had not driven in today, Osley intended riding out there just to see that everything was all right. It had been over a month since Quade had been in, and Osley suspected he knew the reason. Quade never got away from town in under a half-day at best.

153

He waved as the wagon pulled up across the street. No use in going over now, he thought a little grumpily. A man would not be able to get near enough to say hello to the Quades without someone stepping on his toes. See; he was right. Hamilton left off his work of arranging a display and moved toward the wagon. Mowbry came out of his shop, still holding his hammer, and Coniston was coming out of the bank, his face alight. Jim Quade would be the center of a little group, wherever he went in town.

Osley grinned as he watched Quade hand Susan down from the wagon with solicitous care. If he was any judge of signs, Jimmy was going to have a brother before very long. Sure, it was going to be a boy, he told himself Jim Quade could never have anything else but a son. He felt the warmth of pride as he thought of that night, six months ago. Quade had asked him to be his best man. Doc Sanders said he had never seen a man look more silly, and Osley guessed he had been beaming all over his face. But that was a moment for a man to treasure in his memories.

Quade threw back his head and laughed at something one of them said, and his amusement reflected on Osley's face. Quade had changed, too. He could laugh readily these days, and the deep, suspicious bitterness was gone. He acted as though he truly believed he lived among trusting friends. He is, Osley thought. He is.

Mrs. Wilson came down the walk and pushed Hamilton and Mowbry apart, She had a carrying voice, and Osley heard every word she said. She took Susan's elbow, her indignation showing on her red face. "You come with me," she said. "They'd keep you standing out in the sun all day."

Quade said with mock gloom, "Now, I've lost her for another day. She likes to visit you so much, she never knows when to come home."

Osley thought judiciously, he could not have looked as silly as Mrs. Wilson did now. That Quade had a way with people. Mrs. Wilson led Susan away, and the little group broke up. Quade went into the bank with Coniston. Osley nodded with satisfaction. He guessed the negotiations for that land Quade wanted was in the final stages. "That'll hold him with us," he said aloud and grinned. Quade would be the rest of his life paying off that land. It wasn't really the bondage it sounded. Land was a good thing to own, and in the buying of it, a man was building something he could hand to his sons.

Osley leaned back in his chair, his eyes half closed in contentment. As he had thought a few moments earlier, this was a good town with good people in it. And he meant to keep it that way.

He opened his eyes wide at the sound of hoofs from the upper end of the street. He stared at the rider, and a tightness began pulling at his cheeks. The man was a stranger, and even at this distance, Osley thought there was an attitude of seeking about him. Maybe he actually saw it, or maybe it was an instinct. It did not matter which, for it carried its warning.

Osley pulled his pistol out of its holster and laid it in his lap. He covered the gun with the newspaper and waited. He still looked the picture of indolent ease. Only an alert man would have noticed the tightness pulling at his eye corners.

The rider came down the street, his head turning one way, then another as he looked curiously about him. Osley could not put a name to him, but it did not matter. The man came out of a group, and the stamp of it was all over him. Stobie Hobart belonged to that group.

The rider stopped before Osley and looked down at him. He was young—he might have been a year out of his teens but no more. His trappings were on the elegant side, and his clothing was the same. There was a restlessness about him, a dissatisfied seeking, and the bright, hungry gleam in his searching eyes emphasized it.

Osley steadily returned his look. This was the third one in the last eight months, and he wondered if it would ever end. But this man was the first in the last five months, and even discounting the inactivity of the winter months, maybe it was slowing down. It would take patience, a slow wearing away of interest. But new names would be pushing up, replacing Quade's, and one of these days, he would be pushed back into legend, and the current awareness of him would be completely gone.

Damn such young ones as this, Osley thought violently. They were too impatient to build something on their own. They wanted to seize a standing, a reputation already made.

The man said, "Howdy, sheriff," and there was mockery in his tone.

Osley thought bitterly, there's always a mockery, a contempt in them for the established values. They can be taught, he thought with vehemence. There was always danger in the teaching, but it could be done.

"Looking for something?" he asked. It might as well be brought out into the open at once.

"Why, yes," the man drawled. "I heard Jim Quade was living around here."

"Know him?" Osley asked.

The man shook his head. "Just thought I'd like to look him over."

Osley said flatly, "He hasn't carried a gun for eight months."

The gleam in the man's eyes seemed more hungry. "That's right interesting," he said.

"He doesn't have to," Osley said and spilled the paper from his lap. He casually held the gun, not pointing it at the man. He did not miss the thinning of the lips, nor the flaring of the nostrils.

"The Jim Quade you heard of is gone," he said. "You got no interest in this one at all."

The rider leaned forward, and the challenge in his eyes was growing. "That's my business, sheriff."

Osley knew the thoughts running through his mind. A fat, olding man faced him, and even though the man held a pistol, he did not have enough sense to point it. This young one was fast, or he would not be here. Any answer to the challenge in him was a goad, and he was on the verge of demonstrating just how fast he was now.

Osley said calmly, "I wouldn't do that. Just look around you."

The horseman slowly turned his head. Mowbry, across the street, was on the walk, a rifle cradled in his arms. Gillian was standing in front of his store, two doors down, and he pointed a pistol at the man. To his left,

Hamilton stood with a rifle.

"You ride out faster than you came in," Osley said. He caught the flash of resentment in the eyes. "You're a dead man, if you don't." Jim Quade would not like this kind of protection, but he was getting it just the same.

A lash replaced the soft note in Osley's voice. "Don't you think we could spot you? Your kind sticks out like a sore thumb. You, or none like you are bothering Quade." He could have spoken the things Quade had done for this town, and it would mean nothing to this man. All he could understand was a show of power, a determination of violence.

The man said with a sneer, "This Quade can't be so much, to be hiding behind all of you."

"You figure it that way and stay alive," Osley said. "You might kill Jim Quade. But you wouldn't live very long. This town would tear you to pieces. It doesn't want to lose him."

He watched the man struggle with a decision. "Go on," he said. "You'll get no other warning."

The rider lifted his reins. "They'll laugh when I tell them this about the great Quade."

"You tell them," Osley said. It was a small sop the man was carrying away with him. Why not let him have it.

He watched the rider wheel his horse and watched its pace pick up. The canter was a fast gallop by the time he reached the edge of town. He thought the man would not return. He had seen a show of violence, and though he would push and twist it around in his mind, it would still be there. By the time he had gone a few miles, he would talk himself into a victory, a backing-down of Quade. If a man wanted to believe a certain way, no facts could change it.

Osley shook his head at the three townsmen and watched them disappear into their stores. He put away his pistol. That was one more time, and maybe it would be the last.

He picked up his paper, and the sun was comfortably warm on him. Maybe there had been a small element of danger for him in facing that rider. The thought caused him no distress. There was always an element of danger, when a man held onto the worth-while values. There was one danger he would never run again —that of losing his self-respect. He looked across at the bank and grinned. Jim Quade would approve of the way he was thinking.

THE END